UNNATURAL

UNNATURAL

SLOANE BRITAIN

CUTTING EDGE

ISBN-13: 978-1-952138-93-5

Published by
Cutting Edge Books
PO Box 8212
Calabasas, CA 91372
www.cuttingedgebooks.com

CHAPTER ONE

Allison eased herself carefully across the slippery sheets to the edge of the bed. Her feet dangling off the edge, she groped for the floor. She felt the slick, fur-like material of the rug between her toes. For a moment she played with it, enjoying the sensual tickling sensation on her bare foot. Then she sat up slowly, careful not to wake the girl sleeping on the other side of the bed.

That was a mistake.

She'd have to get all the way out of the bed now. There was no turning back. No retreating, brave gentlemen, for the enemy has us surrounded on all sides.

Allison braced herself for the effort of standing up. No good. She couldn't make it. Not just yet anyway. She'd just sit there on the edge of the bed for a few minutes longer working up enough energy to stand upright.

Slowly, I will handle this whole problem slowly, she told herself. If I take my time I'll be able to figure the whole thing out. After all, it's not such a difficult matter. People do it every day. I've done it myself a few thousand times. What's so difficult about getting out of bed in the morning?

I'll do it in steps. First, I will open my eyes.

She concentrated deeply, trying to order each little muscle to do its proper job. At last, they responded. Her lids came up. They scratched and tugged like a boat being pulled across the sand, but at least they moved.

Everything was too bright for a moment. All the colors in the room assaulted her tortured eyes with a tormenting brilliance.

She blinked a few times and then it was all right. The world was more or less the same as it had always been.

It was only about ten steps to the john and once she got there, she'd be all right. She could get under the shower and even though the first few minutes of it would be torture, the freezing water would eventually wash the hangover right out of her.

She braced her feet firmly against the soft rug and ordered her bones to stand up. Just as she eased herself off the bed, one of the springs groaned.

Damn!

Allison glanced at the girl on the other side of the bed. Maybe she hadn't heard it. Maybe she was still asleep.

"Morning, baby." Lydia lay as if still sleeping, her eyes closed.

"I tried not to wake you."

"It's all right. I've been awake for over an hour now. Just lying here thinking." Lydia rolled over on her back. She opened her eyes and looked at Allison and smiled.

Allison stared back at her. Those eyes, so incredibly blue. The light, flower-like blue of innocence.

"Come here."

Allison hesitated. She didn't have to obey the command. She was free, white and over twenty-one. She couldn't be put in jail or deported or anything else if she just turned her back and walked away.

"I said, come here."

Feeling as if her mind were off somewhere else while her body moved with a life of its own, Allison walked around to the other side of the bed. She knelt down and put her hands on Lydia's shoulders.

Lydia raised one eyebrow, amusement twitching the corners of her mouth.

Allison sank to her knees beside the bed. She closed her eyes as her lips found Lydia's. The kiss was long and gentle and familiar from hundreds of other such morning kisses—and no less delicious.

"I love you," Allison whispered.

"I thought for a moment you weren't going to say it," Lydia said. "You know I like to hear you say it. Especially first thing in the morning."

"I love you," Allison repeated.

"And I love you. You were marvelous last night. I love you when you're that way. It was good, wasn't it, darling?"

"Yes."

"See, I told you you'd like it. You just have to relax."

"Yes, I know. And I keep trying to but sometimes I just can't. That's why I had to drink so much first."

"You did have a lot to drink last night. How do you feel?"

"Like death warmed over," Allison replied truthfully.

"Poor baby. Here, you get back in bed and I'll get up and make the coffee this morning."

"No! I'll do it. It's all right. I won't mind."

Allison got up and went out to the kitchen. The shower would have to wait. It was worth enduring her hangover to keep Lydia in bed for a little while longer.

She put a pan of water on the stove to boil and got cups and saucers and a jar of instant coffee down from the cupboard. She had to clear a space on the table with her elbows before setting them down.

Christ, the kitchen was a mess. Thank God she had gotten in there before Lydia. All Lydia would have to see was that sink full of dirty dishes and she'd make life hell for the rest of the week.

There was no reasoning with her. Lydia knew perfectly well that she hadn't had time to clean up last night after dinner but that wouldn't stop her. She'd carry on for days about the mess anyway.

At least by making the coffee herself, Allison might get away with keeping Lydia out of the kitchen until it was all straightened up. She would wait until Lydia was taking her shower and then if she rushed like mad maybe she could get the dishes done and the worst of the clutter out of the way before Lydia saw it.

"Um-m-m," Lydia murmured. "This is good. You know, I can always tell the difference between instant coffee and regular. I wish you'd always use regular coffee in the morning. I like it so much better."

Allison bent her head over her cup to hide her smile. Lydia was such a fool about some things. But if it made her happy to think that she was drinking percolated coffee Allison sure as hell wasn't going to tell her the truth.

When they were finished, Allison piled their dishes on a tray and carried them back to the kitchen. Lydia would be busy for the next half-hour bathing and dressing. It was enough time to get the kitchen back into reasonably presentable shape.

Lydia had an appointment for noon at her hairdresser's. They drove uptown in silence. That is, there was no conversation between them. Lydia directed all her attention to the mid-day traffic. Cars that got in her way or didn't move quickly enough when a traffic light changed were graced with a barrage of curses from Lydia that would have done justice to a stevedore.

It was silly to take the car anyway. They would have gotten there just as fast in a cab and there would be no problem finding a parking spot. As it was, after driving around the side streets for twenty exasperating minutes, they finally had to leave the car in a parking lot.

Lydia's face was white with rage by the time they finally reached the beauty salon. It was childish of her to let a simple thing like not being able to find a place to park get her angry. Yet this was just the sort of thing that drove Lydia wild. She'd calm down in a little while but in the meantime she wasted an awful lot of energy over a trivial frustration. She'd be a perfect bitch until she had worked the anger out of herself. Allison was thankful the hairdresser would be taking Lydia off her hands until she had calmed down.

Allison settled herself down in a chair in the beauty salon's lounge to wait for Lydia. All around her beautiful women were putting on their street clothes and repairing their makeup.

She tried not to stare at them but she kept looking, nevertheless. So many beautiful women. The cream of New York's wealthy women had their hair done here. She could spot most of the women who had money of their own or who had married well. They were the well-groomed ones whose quiet grace expressed perfect self-assurance.

There were others, by far the majority. They were the women whose beauty was almost too perfect to be human. There was something contrived about them. The appearance of an exquisite statue that somehow could move like a living person. These were the high-priced call girls and the kept women of the big-time gangsters.

Allison felt foolish sitting there. Everyone else in the place was either coming for an appointment or leaving after one. She just sat there waiting the two hours until Lydia would be ready to leave.

There were a pile of magazines on a table beside her chair. She picked one up and leafed through it. At least if she were reading she wouldn't look quite so much like an abandoned orphan.

Damn Lydia for making her wait around here like a damn fool. Lydia didn't need her. She could easily have made the trip by herself. And Allison could have put the time to much better use. There were a thousand and one things she could have done with the time she was wasting.

But, of course, Lydia wouldn't hear of it. She would insist, as always, that Allison accompany her everywhere.

Okay, so it was a small price to pay for what she got in return. That was the argument she had been giving herself for nearly a year now and it was starting to wear thin. Lydia made her put up with a lot of nonsense, even made her wait on her as if she were an unemancipated slave, but Lydia paid all the bills. Lydia fed, clothed and sheltered her.

A fair exchange is no robbery and Allison was free to leave at any time she thought that Lydia was making unreasonable demands.

She had often thought of leaving. There were too many times when Lydia made life hell for her. Nothing was worth those hours and days of anguish and despair. Lydia was a sadistic bitch who delighted in tormenting Allison.

But Allison would never leave her.

Allison loved Lydia.

She loved her so much that sometimes she thought it was wrong. Human beings weren't supposed to love each other so much. There must be something sinful about a love so strong it blotted out everything else, including decency and self-respect.

Allison tried hard to fix her attention on the magazine. There was an article in it on the Far East situation. That ought to hold her interest. She read a few paragraphs.

It was no good. She couldn't concentrate. The words ran together and became meaningless. She gave up the attempt and let her thoughts drift back. Back to the time before Lydia.

She had come to New York from a small town in Massachusetts. Ever since she could remember she had wanted to get out of that stifling smalltown atmosphere and live in the big city. At last, the summer when she was twenty years old, she had saved enough money to make the move.

The day of her arrival she found a room in a hotel near Greenwich Village. As soon as her bags were unpacked she headed for famous Washington Square Park.

There, Allison sat on a bench for hours as the light faded from the sky and cool evening breezes chilled her. Her eyes eagerly devoured everything and everybody in the park. Yet, she hadn't really been aware of anything else except the wonder of at last being in New York.

I'm here, she kept repeating to herself. Really here ... in New York. I, Allison Fuller, am sitting on a bench in Washington Square Park in Greenwich Village in the city of New York.

When she finally got up, her body ached from sitting so long. It didn't matter. She was lightheaded with excitement. Walking was like dancing because the pavements were part of New York.

She was sticky with perspiration and her makeup needed refreshing but she didn't want to go back to her hotel. Not yet. She wanted to see more of the city first.

No one noticed her as she walked along the narrow twisting streets. So different from Barton. In the city where she had grown up everyone knew your business. You couldn't go for a walk without having the whole town know it.

She was happy. For the first time in the twenty years of her life she knew what the word happiness meant. It meant freedom.

Maybe it means something else to other people but it meant freedom to Allison Fuller because she had never known it before. Because she had lived with a widowed mother who had watched her every move and had always had plenty to say.

The word for it was nagging. Allison had been nagged about every detail of her appearance, character and behavior. She had been told that she was the worst daughter on earth, that she would never amount to anything.

And she knew her mother was right. She knew it even though she never could quite put her finger on the details. It didn't really matter. Whatever she had done—whether she could remember what it was or not—she was guilty and deserved to be punished.

Only she wished that she could be punished differently. That her mother would hit her instead of using words.

Like the time when she was a little girl. She could understand her mother punishing her that time.

She remembered it so well. As if it were yesterday she remembered how she had gotten out of bed early and tiptoed down the hall. She was going to surprise her parents. That was when her father was still alive. Allison was going to play a joke on Mommy and Daddy and then they'd all laugh about it and Daddy would pick her up in his arms and give her his special hug.

She opened the door to her parent's bedroom carefully, silently. As soon as it was open she would run in and yell "Surprise!"

Only she didn't yell anything. She just stood there with the door open and looked at Mommy and Daddy.

Allison didn't know what they were doing. She didn't understand it and she didn't know any name to give it. All she knew was that she couldn't stop watching them and that it was making her feel all funny inside.

And then her mother had opened her eyes and seen Allison standing in the doorway. Mommy had been mad.

She had gotten out of the bed and she had called Allison names. And then Mommy had picked up a hairbrush and she had spanked Allison with it. She spanked hard and Allison cried. And somehow Allison had known that this was right, that Mommy should spank her because she had been so bad and felt so funny inside.

Her mother had never spanked her again. Instead, she had used words to punish. Allison had grown up with the memory of that spanking as the one time when everything had made sense. Nagging never helped her understand what she had done wrong. She knew that she was always doing something bad but she never understood quite what. She wished that Mommy would stop nagging and spank her again.

But Mommy never did. She spanked Allison just that once and then soon after, her father had died and Mommy never spanked Allison again.

But all that was in the past. It didn't matter any longer. Allison was grown up now and she was in New York and there was no mother or anyone else to punish her for crimes she didn't remember committing.

In the months that followed Allison moved out of the hotel and into an apartment of her own. It wasn't much. Just two rooms and a kitchen on the lower East Side. The neighborhood was straight out of an early George Orwell novel but the rent was low.

She got herself a job with a welfare agency. That job lasted four weeks. When they let her go she was told that her work was satisfactory but the agency just couldn't continue to put up with her frequent absences.

That was the trouble on her next job and the one after that. In three months Allison had been hired and fired from three jobs. Each time for the same reason.

She made an honest effort to get to work. Every morning she got up in plenty of time. It was while she was on her way to work that the trouble started. The headaches would begin with a sharp, shooting pain in her temples. Within minutes she was dizzy and nauseous. She could hardly see, barely managed to walk. It was all she could do to hail a cab and direct the driver to take her back to her apartment.

Sometimes the headaches cleared up in a couple of hours. Other times they went on for days. No matter how she struggled to overcome them and get to work, she was forced to simply lie still on her bed and wait until the headache went away.

Naturally, she consulted a doctor. In time, many doctors; each one reported no physiological basis for the headaches. They pointed out to her the possibility of an emotional origin for her discomfort. Her headaches were what are called migraine headaches and the only cure for them would result from intensive treatment with a specialist.

In other words: get thee to a psychiatrist.

The idea wasn't disturbing. Allison was far too well read and sophisticated to balk at the idea of being psychoanalyzed. Only analysts cost money, a lot of money.

She hadn't had that much money in the bank to begin with and changing jobs every few weeks hadn't given her a chance to save. She was almost broke. Psychoanalysis would have to wait.

More immediately important was the problem of finding a new job. She took the first one that was offered to her.

Working for Steve Callum was horrible. He was a lousy boss, a real bully who made his employees jump for their salaries. He was hated and feared by everyone in the office. The only reason anyone stayed with him was that he paid them more than they could get anywhere else.

Allison was more afraid of him than anyone else. She trembled every time he looked at her. Yet, she was fascinated by him. Attracted would be a more accurate word. For the first time in her life Allison considered the possibility of making love with a married man.

Steve was a shrewd guy. He saw the way Allison went for him. What the hell, why not give it a whirl? What did he have to lose? She was a good-looking girl.

Steve liked the way Allison was built, tall and not too thin. She had good breasts, the kind that stood right up and pointed out at you. Her hips were nice too, round and soft. He always had been a sucker for girls with curly black hair worn shoulder-length. And he liked that look in her green eyes, like a kid who's afraid she's going to be hurt.

Yeah, Allison Fuller might be real good. He'd give it a whirl.

One afternoon Steve asked Allison to stay in the office late. He said he had some letters he wanted her to type up.

Steve stayed in his private office while Allison finished up the typing at her own desk. It took her a long time, she was so nervous she kept making errors and had to re-do a lot of the work. She cursed herself for being childish. There was nothing to get nervous about. But the sound of her typewriter in the deserted office made her quake with terror.

When she finished all the letters, she gathered them up and brought them in to Steve to sign. She hesitated for a moment outside his closed door. She couldn't hear a sound from his office.

I can't do it, Allison thought. I'm going to be sick. I just can't go in there and face him all alone like this. I'll just leave the letters outside his door and go home. Tomorrow I'll call up and tell his secretary I won't be coming in anymore.

She knocked on the door.

"Come in," Steve barked.

She opened the door and walked in, her knees feeling like water. "Mr. Callum, the uh, the letters ... I need ... that is ... they need ... your signature."

"Well, bring them over here. What do you expect me to do, come and get them from you?" he thundered.

She brought the letters over to his desk.

He took them from her. "Sit down," he ordered, indicating a chair.

She sank into the chair and watched him as he signed the letters. What a big man he was! It was all muscle and no fat, Allison knew. Steve's bushy brown hair and thick eyebrows contributed to his appearance of brutal strength. Even the cigar he held clenched between his teeth looked menacing.

Steve finished signing the letters and pushed them over to one side of his desk. He tilted back in his swivel chair and stared at Allison.

"If there's nothing more, I'll be going now, Mr. Callum," she said, starting to rise.

"Sit down," he ordered quietly.

She sat.

He reached behind his desk and pulled open the door of a wall cabinet. Inside was a completely stocked small bar.

"Scotch?"

"Really, Mr. Callum, I don't feel like having a drink. I have a million things to do at home and…" She fell silent under his penetrating stare.

"Scotch?" he asked again.

"Please, on the rocks."

He mixed the drinks, double shots, for both of them and carried them over to the couch.

Allison hesitated. Obviously he intended for her to follow him. She got up and went over to the couch, carefully seating herself as far away from him as she could.

They talked their way through the first two drinks. The conversation was a typical boss-new employee one. He asked her how she liked her job and she lied and told him she loved it. He asked her vague questions about her life which she answered timidly.

When Steve came back to the couch with their third round of drinks, he sat down right next to her. He was so close that she could see the stubble on his talcumed jowls.

"You know, Miss Fuller… May I call you Allison?"

She nodded her consent.

"Good. Call me Steve. You know, Allison, I've been watching you. You've got a good head on your shoulders. Smart. I like a girl who's smart."

"Thank you. I…"

"I've been thinking about you," he interrupted her. "Yes sir, I have. I could use a smart girl around here. No need for you to be stuck out there with all the typists. No sir, not a smart girl like you. You should have more responsibility."

"But I…"

"Now, I could use a smart girl as my personal secretary," he interrupted her again. "Somebody who is real smart and knows how to keep the boss happy."

His hand was on her knee. She stared at the thick black hairs covering the knuckles. She wanted to run, scream, get away from him somehow.

Yet, she could only listen to his words numbly and watch the stealthy progress of his massive hand up her thigh.

His face was next to hers. Steve nuzzled against her hair. He sighed deeply and the acrid smell of cigar smoke on his breath nauseated her.

"I like you," Steve said.

He slipped his arm around her waist and drew her to him. His kiss was wet and slobbery. He seemed not so much to be caressing her lips as chewing on them. Allison nearly gagged as he thrust the length of his tongue into her mouth.

Time was suspended. She couldn't think or move. A voice screamed silently within her, "Let me alone!" Why didn't he listen to the voice and go away?

If he noticed that she wasn't responding, Steve wasn't bothered by it. His breath came in short gasps.

She screamed.

Steve wrenched one hand out from under her and clamped it across her mouth.

He fell on top of her. His body a dead weight of satisfied exhaustion.

When Steve had finally recovered himself sufficiently to move, he sat up on the couch and began straightening up his clothes. Allison pulled herself erect also and huddled herself into a little frightened heap at the end of the couch, as far away from Steve as she could get.

Neither of them spoke. They didn't even look at each other.

At last, Steve sighed deeply and stole a furtive glance at Allison. As he did so, he noticed a still-damp stain. A crimson smear marred the yellow silk couch upholstery.

"Oh my God!" Steve murmured. "I'm sorry. I—I didn't know. If I had only known that you were a virgin …"

Allison said nothing.

Her silence had a disquieting effect on him. He couldn't understand it. What was she thinking? Why didn't she answer him?

"Look," he began angrily, "this is as much your fault as mine. Why didn't you tell me you'd never had it before?"

Allison was silent, her eyes fixed on the rug beneath her feet.

"Come on, let's get out of here," Steve continued. "I've got to get home. My wife's expecting me. She'll have a fit because I'm so late already."

He stood up. Allison didn't move. Steve reached down and took her hands in his, pulling her to her feet.

"Look, you run along now," he said, "I've got to make a couple of phone calls before I leave."

She started walking wordlessly toward the door.

Steve ran to catch up with her just before she got on the elevator.

"You better take a cab home," he said, thrusting a twenty dollar bill toward her.

Allison looked at the money as if she couldn't understand what it was.

He dug deeper into his pocket and came out with a roll of bills. He peeled a few off the roll, crumpled them up and thrust them into her coat pocket.

"That'll keep you going for awhile," Steve said. He looked away from her as he spoke, unable to tolerate the vacant, bewildered expression in her eyes. "Get yourself another job, will you? I mean, I guess you won't want to be coming back here anymore."

"I understand," Allison murmured. Then she got on the elevator and the door closed behind her.

CHAPTER TWO

The headache didn't begin immediately. For a long while after that night with Steve Callum, Allison existed in a numb limbo world without thought or feeling.

Only one idea kept coming back to her: it had hurt so badly.

All her life she had wondered about men, thought about what it would be like. She had known that someday she would lie in a man's arms and he would teach her all about the great mystery. She had longed for the time when she could learn the great truth.

He had hurt her.

This was what men and women lived and died for. People said that sex was what made the world go round. Women gave up everything which had been important to them for the love of a man.

And it had been pain and nothing else.

For over a week she lay on her bed in the darkened bedroom and thought about this. There was no answer. It should have been wonderful and instead it had been horrible. Something was wrong. She didn't know exactly what.

One night she dreamed that she was alone with Steve Callum again. Only this time it was she who was making the advances. At first he was reluctant and only gradually did she evoke a response in him.

They made love on a big bed that seemed bigger than any room she had ever seen.

There was someone else in the room. A woman was laughing. It was her mother, laughing hysterically at the ridiculous sight of Allison making love to a man.

Her laughter increased in tempo. It had a rhythm to it, a fast staccato of hilarity.

Her mother's laughter had a note of mocking cruelty in it. It was a whip driving them on to more frenzied love-making with each peal.

Allison looked at her mother. She had never seen her look so beautiful as she did then, her face lit up with delight. Suddenly, her mother's expression changed to a dark scowl.

When she looked up again, her mother was gone.

When Allison woke up her first thought was that her mother was hiding somewhere in the bedroom. She had only to search for her.

As the mists of sleep cleared out of her mind, Allison experienced one of those moments of absolute clarity which came with such frightening force they terrified her. Often, just when she awoke or just before falling asleep, her thoughts would suddenly become very clear and she would understand all manner of things.

This morning, she opened her eyes and stared at the edge of sunlight peeping around the drawn window blind. She was afraid, Allison thought. She laughed because she was afraid. I was taking him away from her and she treated it as a joke. But when it got serious, when we were too close, her fright turned to anger.

I should have stopped then, but I didn't. I went on even though I knew how she felt. And because I was bad, Mommy punished me by going away. And after she left, Steve wasn't there any more either. I was all alone.

I'll go to her and tell her I'm sorry. I'll tell her I'll never be bad again. Then maybe I can get her back. She'll yell at me but if

I'm good and don't answer her back, it will be all right again. And maybe if I'm real good she'll punish me without words.

The telephone rang. It was Steve, calling to find out if she was all right.

For a moment she couldn't understand what he was asking her. Who was this who was interrupting thoughts of her mother, driving her away? What did he want with her?

Yes, she told him, she was fine…and please don't bother calling again.

Damn Steve for calling and interrupting her reverie. And damn him for making her aware again of him as a real human being. Damn him a thousand times more for trying to be nice and, by inquiring about her, forcing her to admit that she was all right, that nothing so devastating had actually happened.

Allison had been living on coffee and canned goods, not leaving her apartment since the night she spent with Steve. Now she suddenly felt like being among people again, walking in the fresh air.

She dressed and prepared to go out. As she put on her coat, she felt the bulge in her pocket. She took the money out and counted it for the first time. One hundred dollars. Well, that was nice of the s.o.b.

The morning streets were crowded with people hurrying to work. Allison stood in front of her building watching them go by. What a delicious feeling it was to know she didn't have to join them in their mad rushing toward jobs they hated.

She had the whole day to herself. Tomorrow or even the day after that she could look for work. In the meantime, Steve's hundred dollars could be spent any way she chose.

She could go shopping for some badly needed new clothes or go to a movie or a museum or just about anything. Allison decided that nothing would please her more than a walk around Greenwich Village.

Her route took her through crowded streets of tenements where fruit was hawked in open-air stalls, rotten fruit and discarded peelings spilling out onto the cracked pavements.

There was the factory district where the narrow sidewalks were blocked by huge trucks, their noses sniffing at each other across the streets, their rear ends flung open and inviting toward the stiff-lipped loading platforms.

Allison had to walk mostly in the roadway in this district, dodging the oncoming traffic by stepping close to the parked trucks. The drivers called out to her pleasantly, lascivious intentions couched in pleasantries about the weather. Allison responded to them gaily, never slackening her pace as she replied. Oh, it was nice that strangers could talk to each other this way. And it was a lovely morning, bright and crisp. And she was so pleased with herself because she was young and her body could feel such pleasure in a simple walk through crowded streets.

She sat on a bench in Washington Square Park. She hadn't done that since her first day in New York City. It was so different now. Before, the magic had been there because the city was new and unknown. Today, it still held an element of magic but this was because she now felt herself to be a New Yorker. And this meant that the city belonged to her in a funny kind of way. And the people passing by were her people.

There were shabbily dressed men lounging on some of the benches, their attitude one of relaxation while their eyes ceaselessly kept on the alert for policemen. In the playground, children swung on swings and shrieked delightedly down the chute-a-chute. Their young mothers gathered in groups to exchange neighborhood gossip, their brightly colored toreador pants and jackets a commercial splotch against the solemn grey facades of New York University.

Allison watched the men and women walking their dogs in the park. Two girls came walking past her. One had a huge black Afghan Hound on a leash and the other a Beagle puppy. They took the dogs over to a grassy spot and released them. The Beagle immediately began playing frantically, chasing the obliging Afghan around the park. The Afghan could have crushed the little Beagle with one stroke of his massive paw but instead, he indulged the puppy's presumptuousness.

It was good to sit in the park and funny to watch the two dogs at play and nice to have the whole day free to do with as she pleased. Allison let her head fall back against the back of the bench. She stared up at the browning leaves of the trees. They whispered together in the stirrings of the light breeze.

One so seldom watched the leaves in New York. There were so few trees and one never seemed to have time enough to just sit and look at them.

She remembered the trees in Barton. There had been a small park near her home with magnificent clumps of trees. She used to like to walk under those trees in the fall and shuffle her feet through the fallen leaves.

When she was a little girl she hadn't been allowed to go to the park alone. Her mother had taken her. Every Sunday afternoon, after her housework was finished, Mrs. Fuller took Allison for a walk in the park. After her husband died, Mrs. Fuller had had to go to work and Sunday was the only time she had to spend with her daughter.

By the time they reached the park, Mrs. Fuller's legs would be bothering her. They'd have to sit down for a while before continuing their walk. Allison would force herself to sit still on the bench beside her mother even though her young body was jumping with aliveness inside and she longed to run singing under the trees.

Allison would lean her head back on the bench as she was doing now while her mother talked. She would try to concentrate on the shifting patterns the leaves made and not hear what her mother was saying.

Mrs. Fuller never let an opportunity pass to do what she considered her duty. Now she had Allison alone with her for a whole afternoon. There was a week's silence to make up for. What was a mother for if not to tell her daughter about her faults and steer her in the right direction?

The voice would drone on in Allison's ears. "Why do you have to sit like that?" "Can't you straighten up?" and "You're going to make yourself all round-shouldered." and "Sit straight, I said. Didn't you hear me the first time?" and "Honestly, Allison, I don't know what's to become of you. Seems I talk and talk but you won't change your ways." and "Must you get yourself so dirty? I only put that dress on you an hour ago and look at it already, wrinkled and spotted like a ragamuffin's." And on and on with a thousand and one criticisms expressed in a million and one ways.

By the time her mother felt rested and they could continue their walk, Allison had lost all heart for it. The trees were no longer beautiful. They were big things that just stood there and made silly noises when the wind blew through their leaves and they could stand like that a million years and they'd never care about anything or anybody except themselves.

It wasn't good for her to remember things like that, Allison knew. Yet she couldn't manage to stop the flood of memories that surged in on her.

The inevitable happened. She felt a spot about the size of a dime begin to throb in her right temple. It was painful but isolated and therefore bearable. She could never tell if the headache would stop right there or go on to become a paralyzing nightmare.

Allison looked in her purse for the tranquilizers the doctor had prescribed. If she took one in time it sometimes kept the headaches from getting worse.

Goddamn! She had forgotten to take them along!

But something must be done ... and soon. She could feel the first waves of nausea in the pit of her stomach.

She got off the bench and began walking toward MacDougal Street. She walked slowly, stepping gently, trying not to jar her aching head. At least, if she could reach MacDougal Street before the headache got really bad, there might be a chance for her. A couple of times before she had found that liquor helped. Sometimes it did and sometimes it didn't. Pray God that this time it would.

Focusing was already difficult by the time she reached the corner of MacDougal and West Third Streets. There was a bar on the corner. The stucco walls were painted a brilliant yellow which hurt her eyes. She could dimly make out the sign: El Nuevo Bar. Thank Bacchus, the bar was open for business.

Inside, it was dimly lit and quiet. The sharp odor of the previous night's Spanish cooking hung in the air.

There were only three other people in the bar, two working-men in overalls and, in a corner at the far end of the shadowy room, a woman. Allison made them out dimly, her eyes had almost completely lost ability to focus by now.

She found her way to the bar and pressed herself against its cool mahogany rim. There was an empty stool next to her. She felt too weak to continue standing but she knew that her sense of balance was gone; she would never make it up onto the stool.

"What'll ya have, Lady?" the bartender asked.

"Drink ... I need a drink."

"Yeah, but what?"

"Brandy," she answered him, naming the first thing that came into her mind. "Make it a double," she called to the bartender after he had turned away.

Her hands were shaking so badly she could hardly lift the glass. Almost half of the brandy slopped over the bar.

She ordered another double.

Her hands were steadier. This one went down all right. It even tasted good, raw on her throat but smokily good as it rolled over her tongue.

The liquor hit her stomach like a rain of red hot pebbles. The first drink mingled with the second and her insides lurched.

Allison stood perfectly still, waiting for the intestinal tidal wave to subside. No wonder the liquor was hitting her so quickly, Allison couldn't remember when she had eaten last.

When she felt a little better, she ordered another brandy. If two had been good, three would probably be even better.

She sipped the third drink slowly, looking around the bar and taking it and its inhabitants in for the first time. Her nausea was completely gone, all that remained was a slight, throbbing headache. It was nothing excessive any more, just the usual discomfort of an ordinary headache.

Now that she could focus her eyes better, Allison saw that the two men at the bar were middle-aged construction workers, their overalls powdery with brick dust. They drank their beers in silence, quickly, not looking further than the bull-fight mural behind the bar.

Far to Allison's left, at the curved end of the bar, the woman was watching Allison. Her gaze was unwavering. Even as she lifted the highball glass to her lips, she continued staring at Allison.

The nerve of her! Who the hell did she think she was? The gall of some people! She could at least have the courtesy to be subtle.

Allison couldn't stop herself from staring back at the woman. She didn't want to. The best way to handle discourtesy like hers was to ignore it. Yet, Allison couldn't tear her eyes away.

There was something compelling about her. She was beautiful, yes. Yet there was something about her—an indefinable extra something.

The woman at the end of the bar had pale blonde hair worn shoulder-length. It was straight, the ends curling softly above her collar. She was fair-complexioned, the muted pink and cream of an advertisement for Yardley cosmetics. The light blue of her eyes was heightened to a disconcerting brilliance by the lightness of her skin and hair.

She was wearing a belted camel's hair coat. The coat was exquisitely right for her. It was softly tailored, the epitome of the expensive tailor's ability to construct a simple garment which fairly reeked of tasteful style.

A huge black Doberman pinscher lay curled at her feet. The dog was part of the picture also, almost as if the woman had chosen such a dog as she would a piece of jewelry: to complete her costume.

The woman's stare was swiftly driving Allison straight out of her mind. It made her feel terribly self-conscious. For no logical reason, the woman was making her feel foolish. She felt as if she were acting a part on stage and muffing her lines.

Allison wanted to leave. She felt all right now, her headache was all gone and the liquor no longer tasted good to her. There was no pleasure in anything while the woman held her with that taunting stare.

Allison ordered another drink. She didn't want it but she needed to hold the glass in her hands. She was too nervous to just sit at the bar without drinking. And the thought of walking out of the bar, with the woman observing every line and curve of her body, was unbearable.

Allison was on her fifth double brandy, resolutely staring at the polished gloss of the mahogany bar in order to avoid the woman's gaze, when she felt something wet and cold against her leg. She looked down.

The Doberman was standing next to her, his nose pressed against her calf. The woman was standing behind the Doberman. She looked as if she had been standing there for some time.

Allison returned the steady scrutiny of the ice-blue eyes. The woman didn't so much as wink. Her expression remained set, not smiling, inscrutable.

"Come," the woman said.

No thoughts passed through Allison's mind. Yet she felt as though she understood. As if this moment were the revelation to a great mystery whose presence she had never suspected.

Wordlessly, Allison laid a bill down on the bar to pay for her drinks. She shrugged herself into her coat and picked up her purse.

"My name is Lydia," the woman said as they left the bar.

CHAPTER THREE

Lydia finished with the hairdresser and rejoined Allison in the lounge of the beauty salon. Allison saw her as she stepped off the elevator and came walking toward her.

Not yet completely oriented to the present, still half living in her memories, Allison saw Lydia with the eyes of a stranger. When people know each other well, they seldom really see each other. The visual impression is already formed in the mind; reality of the moment is a matter of trifling changes in detail.

There was a splendor about Lydia as she walked through the rose and gold reception room. She moved as though her Doberman were speeding her along with impatient tugs on the leash.

Her head was held high and tilted slightly backward, an attitude at once zestful and imperious. The corners of her mouth were drawn up ever so slightly in a faint smile. It was an inner laugh of defiance and anticipated triumph.

The other women in the lounge noticed her too. As she came into their midst, each of them stopped whatever she had been doing to stare at her.

There were other women there more beautiful than Lydia. Yet they too were impressed by her. It was perhaps the air of command, of assumed control which set her apart.

Allison saw the look of admiration and envy in the women's eyes. A hundred times before she had seen Lydia evoke this reaction and still her response to it was the same. Allison felt a thrill of pleasure course through her.

This is the woman who has chosen me for her most intimate friend, she wanted to tell everyone. This woman shares everything with me, her home, her pleasures, her bed. I belong to her. The woman you are all admiring is married to me in a union that is beyond any ritualized ceremony.

This is the woman I love.

In the car, driving home, Lydia told her of the plans for the day.

It was always like this. Lydia decided on a program for both of them, arranged for it and only when the moment was almost upon them, told Allison about it.

If Allison objected at all, it was feebly. What good would it do her to object? If she refused to go along, Lydia would permit her to stay at home while she pursued her pleasure alone. And nothing was worse than being away from Lydia, imagining her alone with someone else, twisting and turning with passion in someone else's arms.

"We're having company tonight," Lydia announced.

"Anyone I know?"

Lydia laughed lightly. "You have as much gift for offhanded sarcasm as a bulldozer, darling. Anyway, you don't know him. I hardly do either.

"He's a wholesale grocer I met some years ago. I ran into him the other day when I was at the bank and I invited him up for tonight. His name is Max."

"Thanks for the information," Allison replied. "Now I know exactly what to expect."

"Almost, knowing me," Lydia agreed. "As I've said, I hardly know Max myself. I met him at a party years ago and haven't seen him since. I can tell you that he's Russian and talks like a movie director. One of those professional Russians, you know.

"And I can tell you that Max is a business man who works hard all day and likes to relax in the evening. He'll expect us to entertain him."

"With tea and poetry recitals, no doubt."

Lydia laughed delightedly. "I knew you'd get the picture."

"One thing more," Lydia added as she was parking the car in front of their home, "Max is going to pay us for his evening's entertainment. I'm sure you'll see to it that he gets his money's worth, won't you, darling?"

All through dinner Allison paid more attention to the wine than she did to the food. If only she could get herself really plastered!

The wine was too weak. She finished dinner still conscious. The snifters of cognac Lydia passed around afterward didn't do the trick either. And she couldn't insult their guest by getting herself a bigger drink when he was so obviously anxious to get on to other things.

What a colossal bore he was! Lydia had brought home some dreadful characters before but this one took the cake! Maybe if she had had enough to drink, Allison could have tolerated him. This way, only slightly less than sober, he revolted her.

Lydia, always the stage manager, directed the action subtly at first. She began by asking Allison to call the cleaner's to see if her dress was ready.

The French doors separating the living room from the bedroom were open. Lydia indicated with a nod of her head that Allison was to use the bedroom extension telephone.

Feeling like an actress in an unconvincing play, Allison followed Lydia's directions. She sat down on the bed while she made the phone call as she knew Lydia had wanted her to do.

It was all so ridiculous. The phone call was a ruse, of course. They both knew the cleaners would be closed at this hour. Still, Allison dialed the number obediently and let it ring a long time before announcing that there was no answer.

Lydia came into the bedroom and sat down on the bed next to Allison. She put her arm around Allison's waist.

It was as though they were alone. Yet Allison knew that they were both highly aware of Max watching them from the living room. That was supposed to be the kick in it.

"Max, would you bring me a cigarette?" Lydia called.

Max came scurrying into the room, his beady eyes alight with excitement.

Lydia accepted the cigarette and light he proffered and then gestured to him to sit down. He chose the bench in front of the vanity table. From where he sat, Max had a front row view of the bed. The two girls could see themselves as he saw them in their reflection in the vanity table's mirror.

Lydia puffed contentedly on her cigarette. When it was half-smoked, she held it against Allison's lips so that she could take a puff.

"Share it with me," Lydia whispered as she tightened her embrace and brought her lips to Allison's.

They kissed with open mouths. Lydia exhaled slowly, letting the cigarette smoke filter from her mouth into Allison's.

The effect was instantaneous. She felt as if she were drunk at last. Her head seemed light and somehow not quite connected with her body. Hyperventilation, Allison thought briefly to herself. But the sensation was too intoxicating to be labeled and dismissed.

Bracing herself with one arm against the bed and still keeping the other around Allison's waist, Lydia leaned back. She finished the cigarette slowly, as if it were the most absorbing thing she could occupy herself with at the moment.

Max sat motionless, his body inclined forward in an attitude of painfully-suppressed excitement. His eyes were brimming with water. He kept licking his lips with the tip of his mottled pink tongue.

Lydia finished her cigarette. She leaned across Allison to stub it out in the ashtray on the nighttable. Instead of returning to her former position, however, she brought her head up only until it was on a level with the other girl's.

This time the kiss was forceful and demanding. She pressed herself against Allison, pushing her down until they were lying on the bed.

"Oh, I like this," Max whispered huskily. Now he was standing next to the bed looking down at them. "I like to see two ladies loving each other. You're good girls."

Lydia kept her mouth on Allison's while she opened the buttons of Allison's blouse with her free hand. Allison felt a rush of cool air prickling her skin as her blouse came open.

Then Lydia rocked back a little so that Allison could arch her back off the bed. Max eagerly helped her ease the blouse completely off. While he was at it, he also unhooked her bra. Lydia pulled that off from the front.

"You like this too, Max?" Lydia asked.

"Yes," he hissed.

"So do I, Max," Lydia laughed as she moved so that he couldn't touch Allison.

Allison felt the familiar dream-like heaviness come over her. It felt so good. It would feel even better... If only Max weren't there.

Max slid his hand between them.

"You like that too, Max?" Lydia taunted.

"It's good," he whispered huskily. "Very good."

"You want more?" Lydia continued. "Tell me, Max, how much do you want something more?"

"Fifty dollars."

"Do me a favor, Max darling, and go straight to the devil," Lydia replied in a pleasant, even voice.

"All right, all right … seventy-five."

"A hundred fifty."

"No! That's too much!"

Lydia started her hips swaying, sensuously.

"Okay, a hundred," Max said weakly.

"One hundred twenty-five," Lydia said, "or nothing."

Max sucked his breath in. A terrible struggle was going on in his mind.

"Come on, Max, I'm getting bored with this," Lydia said with peevish annoyance.

"A hundred twenty-five and not a cent more."

In answer, both girls stood up and began taking their clothes off. The bargain was made.

Max took off his trousers and shoes only. Allison was glad of this. He was repulsive enough without her having to see him naked. As aroused as she was, if they didn't get this over with soon she knew she would get sick to her stomach.

He took Allison on first. It didn't hurt. It was just, well, sort of nothing. She could feel him, the nerves responded to his movements. But the sensation stopped right there. There was no building up, no heightening excitement.

Lydia put her mouth next to Allison's ear and whispered softly, "Now."

Allison shook her head. She mouthed the words "I can't."

Lydia frowned. She couldn't understand this about Allison and it annoyed her. But there was time enough for them to fight about it when they were alone.

Lydia slid her hand down between Max and Allison.

"Now … for me," Lydia whispered.

For Lydia, Allison thought as her lover's hand sent explosive shocks of pleasure up her spine.

CHAPTER FOUR

Lydia was already in bed by the time Allison finished straightening up the kitchen. She undressed quickly and got in on her side of the bed.

Lydia reached out one arm and drew Allison close to her. They lay side by side, Lydia in back. She flung one arm over Allison and cupped her breast gently. That was their favorite position for sleeping. The "spoon position" they called it.

"...love..." Lydia murmured sleepily. It was a complete sentence but the rest was mumbled and only the word love came out clearly. She could have asked, as she so frequently did, "Do you love me?" or "Tell me you love me." or Lydia might even have said "I love you."

Allison didn't bother replying. There was no need to. If she had been actually awake at all, Lydia was now sound asleep. She breathed deeply and evenly, with the innocent contentment of a child.

Allison lay next to her, listening to her breathing. Why couldn't she just forget everything and fall asleep when she was tired the way Lydia could? But no, she had to lie awake night after night thinking all kinds of thoughts. Sleep only came after hours of patient waiting.

This night her thoughts wandered back to the same subject she had been occupied with that afternoon. She picked up the thread of her memories.

They had left the bar and walked the few blocks to Lydia's apartment on Greenwich Avenue. It was a walkup building and

Lydia lived on the top floor. There were four steep flights of stairs to climb before they finally reached their destination.

It was quite an apartment. Lydia had the whole floor to herself. There were four spacious rooms separated by French doors. It was furnished in a queer combination of Early American and Swedish modern.

Lydia made coffee and added a liberal dash of cognac to each cup. Allison glanced at her watch. It was only noon. Oh well, what difference did it make? So she would be drunk by noon and maybe something else by dark.

They sat in Lydia's living room drinking coffee and cognac and talking. They talked and talked. It grew dark in the room and they had to turn a lamp on. And still they talked. God, how they talked in those days! About everything and anything.

Lydia told her about herself. She had been married, unhappily, for two years. That union had ended six years ago.

Lydia's husband was a labor leader. She described him as a very idealistic man. Back in the thirties when it was all the rage, he had been a member of the Communist Party. That phase of his life was long past but if knowledge of his previous affiliations ever became widespread, his career would be wrecked.

Lydia admitted that she blackmailed him about this. With complete candor she said, "You must think I'm an utter bastard. Guess I am. It works, though. I've got him so terrified that I might spill the beans, that the poor sucker shells out a fortune in alimony to me willingly. He'd give me anything I wanted to keep me quiet."

She lived off her alimony. The other means of making money—the ways that Allison wasn't to find out about until much later—were strictly for what Lydia called "Kicks".

Allison told Lydia all about herself also. It was funny, never before had she known anyone who made her want to tell them everything. With Lydia she found herself talking about every intimate thing in her life. She told her about her mother and about Steve Callum.

"The bastard," Lydia said when she heard about the way Steve had hurt her. "They're all like that. All they want to do is use a woman for their own pleasure."

A thought came to Allison, an idea about Lydia which had been half-formed in the back of her mind since they had met. She dismissed it quickly. No, it couldn't be. Lydia had been married. Besides, she was so feminine looking.

"I like to drink a lot," Lydia said. "Do you?"

Allison had never before met anyone so completely honest. Lydia's candor was disarming. The things she admitted to doing were wrong, yet there was nothing Allison could say about them. Lydia admitted her guilt and made it quite clear she fully intended to continue as she had been. There was just no kind of answer for an attitude like hers.

For some reason, even though she had had many cups of coffee laced with cognac that day and night, Allison remained completely sober. Lydia also didn't show any signs of drunkenness. Later Allison learned that Lydia almost never did. She could drink like a fish—and frequently did—yet appear completely sober.

There were other times, though. The infrequent occasions when Lydia would drink past that invisible barrier of too much. Those were the times when she became ugly. With *too* many drinks under her belt Lydia got strange ideas. She accused people of all kinds of plots against her. Nobody loved her, she claimed. Everybody she knew, man or woman, was trying to take advantage of her. She accused everyone, including Allison, of concocting elaborate schemes to get things from her.

Sometimes she became violent. Since Allison was the closest person to her, she was usually the object of Lydia's attacks. It was a good thing that Allison was exceptionally strong. She was able to hold Lydia off until her drunken rage passed.

Lydia never remembered anything about the preceding night when she awoke.

It got to be very late. Allison thought about leaving many times. She knew she was being inexcusably impolite. Here she was visiting Lydia for the first time and staying for hours. Yet she couldn't ever seem to work herself up to going.

She wanted to continue their conversation. To sit in Lydia's apartment and listen to everything the older woman had to say.

Outside it was cold and dark and lonely. Here, in Lydia's apartment, she was surrounded by warmth, graciousness and charm. And Lydia was so nice to her, so attentive to her every need. And such a charming, stimulating conversationalist also.

Prufrock, the Doberman, stood in front of the door and whined. He looked at Lydia beseechingly.

Lydia smiled ruefully. "Don't ever become a mother," she cautioned Allison. "I love the damn dog but there are times when I feel like wringing his lovely neck. And this is one of them."

She got up off the chair where she had been sitting and went to the closet to get her coat and the dog's leash.

"I'll take him out," Allison offered.

"No, thanks," Lydia replied. "He's not used to you and might give you trouble. I don't really mind taking him out. The walk will do me good. I'm all stiff from sitting so long. Wait here for me, will you? I won't be gone long."

"It's getting late. I think I had better go home."

"No, don't. I'll be in the mood for another cup of coffee when I get back and you can keep me company."

"All right," Allison agreed. "But the least I can do is wash these cups and saucers for you while you're gone."

An amused smile flickered over Lydia's face. "You're an exceptional guest. Offering to walk my dog and then to wash my dishes ... that's what I call real nice. I think I'm going to like knowing you, Allison. Yes, I think we'll get along very well."

"Give up all thoughts of going home tonight. You're staying here," Lydia announced. She came into the living room with the dog. "Just look at us! It's raining torrents out there. I'm soaked to the skin. You're not going out in that weather, young lady."

"Well, if I wouldn't be too much trouble. I don't want to be a nuisance."

"Nonsense. Plenty of room for you here. I don't want to hear another word about it." Lydia unbuttoned her coat and dramatically wrung a sleeve. It dripped a small puddle of water onto the floor.

"I better get out of these clothes," Lydia said. "And I'll need a real hot bath to take the chill out of my bones. Allison, would you make some fresh coffee for us? Bring it in to me when it's ready. I'll be in the bath."

Instead of going somewhere else to undress, Lydia followed Allison out to the kitchen and disrobed there while Allison made a fresh pot of coffee.

Allison couldn't help seeing her. As Lydia took her clothes off, Allison saw that she had a gorgeous body. By conventional standards, Lydia was a little overweight. She had none of the lean, flat look so prized these days.

Instead, Lydia looked like a beauty of yesteryear. Her body was lush, like a Reuben's painting. Her waist was minute, an ultra-feminine indentation below which her hips swelled out in rounded loveliness.

Her breasts were large and firm and spaced far apart. Lydia's shoulders were a trifle too broad but her hips were wide enough so that she didn't look unbalanced.

Her skin was flawless, the same soft pink and cream as her face. She stood in front of Allison completely nude, her firmly muscled legs apart. Her head was held high and inclined backward, her pale gold hair seeming to flow richly down to her shoulders. She looks like a Valkyrie, Allison thought.

Allison appreciated the beauty of Lydia's body as she would a painting. There was no embarrassment, she felt as free to look at her as she would at a statue. Lydia evidently felt no need for privacy either.

"You don't know how much I envy you," Allison said. "You're beautiful and you have all this," she indicated the attractive apartment. "I wish I had half as much as you do."

Lydia's face clouded over. "Don't envy me, Allison. I'm not always the blissfully happy fool you think I am."

"I didn't mean it that way." Something had gone wrong somehow. Confusion had crept into the conversation. She hadn't meant that she thought Lydia was some kind of happy idiot without a care in the world.

If only Lydia wouldn't just stand there like that. It was uncomfortable carrying on a conversation with someone who was naked. Allison couldn't understand such a complete lack of inhibitions.

"I meant that you seem to have all the superficial things a woman could want: a beautiful home, freedom and all the money you need," Allison tried to explain. "And you're so lovely you could attract just about any man."

"I know that's what you meant," Lydia said. She gathered her clothes up in a bundle and started to walk out of the kitchen. "Just remember one little thing, Allison: One person's ambrosia is another's chopped liver."

Now that was a hell of a way of expressing it! Allison felt more uncomfortable than ever. Why had Lydia said that as if she were making an extremely important point?

"What if you happen to like chopped liver?" Allison called out.

Lydia came back and stuck her head around the corner of the door. "Do you?" she asked.

"Do I what?"

"Like chopped liver."

"As a matter of fact, I do. Is that bad?"

"On the contrary," Lydia laughed, "It's very good. Especially if you like it with onions, raw ones." With that, she winked broadly and left the room again.

Allison gave up trying to fathom Lydia's meaning. Surrealistic conversations were not her forte.

She poured the coffee into two cups, put them on a tray and carried them into the bathroom after Lydia.

Lydia was just getting into the tub. She motioned to Allison to seat herself on the closed lid of the john. Allison watched Lydia lower herself slowly into the tub. She lay back and shut her eyes. The water lapped against her breasts gently.

While Lydia was soaping herself, Allison thought about her. She was such an unusual person. Why had Lydia taken her remark so seriously? Was she really very unhappy? She had everything. What could be troubling her so much?

Allison glanced at the bedroom, visible through the opened bathroom door. It was certainly a room designed for love-making as well as sleep. It was softly lighted, the bed was outsized and comfortable looking. A thick carpet cushioned the floor.

Even the items on the vanity table contributed to the impression. The top was littered with bottles and jars of cosmetics and perfumes. Lydia had all the equipment for making herself attractive to men. But if that wasn't what she wanted, what she needed to make her happy, what did she need? Why did she take such care with her appearance? Who was she trying to attract?

She handed Lydia a cup of coffee wordlessly and returned to her seat. Allison hoped there wouldn't be any more conversation for a few minutes. She needed a few minutes to think. Something new had entered into the evening and she couldn't quite figure out what it was.

Lydia was making her feel tense and uncomfortable. It was silly of her to feel that way, childish really. Yet Lydia made her want to say profound things, make witty jokes, show off. She wanted Lydia to like her. Wanted it desperately.

Lydia finished with her coffee and extended the cup to Allison who took it and placed it beside her own on the window ledge.

"Scrub my back for me, will you?"

It was a thoroughly reasonable request. Allison took the washcloth and soaped it well. She rubbed it gently all over Lydia's satiny back.

"Um-m-m-m," Lydia sighed in exaggerated bliss.

Touching Lydia was disturbing. Allison felt a strange response growing within her. She wondered what it would be like if she dropped the washcloth and touched Lydia's smooth skin with her own hands. Was it really as soft and silken feeling as it looked?

Of course she would do no such thing. She continued scrubbing Lydia's back with the washcloth.

Lydia finished with her bath and got into a pair of tailored cotton pajamas. They went back out to the living room for one last cognac.

Allison parted the drapes and looked out the window. The rain was coming down in sheets. A howling wind was lashing it against the pane.

"I'm glad you asked me to stay," she said as she turned away from the window. "It's horrible out there."

"I'm glad, too," Lydia said, handing her a drink.

Allison stretched out on the couch. It was so warm and quiet in the apartment. She took a sip of cognac. "This is the life. I love it here. I could stay forever.

"This has been a wonderful day. I like being with you, Lydia."

Lydia's face was hidden behind swirls of smoke from her cigarette. Allison couldn't see her expression as she replied in a low voice, "And I like having you."

Much later, when they had finished their drinks, Lydia said, "I think we'd better get to bed."

Allison was tired, she felt heavy with sleep. Yet she didn't want to go to bed. Not yet. She wanted to stay up talking some more. Maybe that way she would learn more about Lydia and why such a fascinating, beautiful woman had taken this sudden interest in her.

Lydia handed her a pair of pajamas.

Allison never wore pajamas. She preferred to sleep in the nude. Still, she couldn't very well do that when she was a guest in someone else's home.

She followed Lydia into the bedroom. Lydia unzipped the zipper on the back of her dress for her. Then she fussed about getting slippers and a robe for Allison.

It was nice being waited on this way. Still, it made Allison a little uncomfortable. More than that, she wished that Lydia would leave the room while she undressed. It was all right for her if she didn't mind being seen naked but Allison was embarrassed by it.

"If you'll give me some sheets and a pillow I'll make up the couch," Allison called out after she had the pajamas on.

"Don't be silly, my bed's big enough for both of us."

No denying that. But Allison found the prospect unnerving. Her mouth was dry and she could feel a fluttery sensation in her diaphragm.

Allison got into bed first. She tried to stay awake until Lydia returned from checking the door lock but the bed was too comfortable and she was too tired.

She awoke a little later from a bad dream. Her mother had been at it again; listing all her faults maddeningly. Allison woke up with a start.

Her mother had been saying something, something very important. But Allison couldn't remember what it was. If she could only remember what it was her mother had been saying. It had been the key to everything. Her mother had finally told her what it was she had done, the thing that made her feel so guilty. Only that was in the dream and awake, Allison had no idea of what it was. All she knew was that she had been bad in some way and deserved to be punished for it.

She could feel Lydia's presence next to her in the bed. The nearness of her body made Allison feel calmer, more secure.

Allison thought about what it would be like to lie with Lydia's arm around her. It would be comforting. She would feel warm and protected. But Lydia was asleep and Allison didn't want to disturb her and besides, it was a childish idea.

She moved just a little closer to Lydia in the bed. She was so close that every time Lydia exhaled her breath caressed Allison's cheek.

That was nice.

She could go back to sleep now.

The next day they went for a drive. It was a fine, clear, fall day. The sun was out and all the colors shone brightly as if washed by last night's rain.

Lydia drove too fast. It took Allison a long while before she could stop worrying about having an accident and start paying attention to the scenery.

They drove to Westport, Connecticut. Lydia had spent most of her childhood there, only coming to New York after her marriage.

Lydia took her on the grand tour of Westport. She pointed out the schools she had attended, the places where she used to live and the country club she had belonged to.

It was very impressive. Impressive because Lydia obviously came from a very wealthy family. That sort of thing didn't mean anything really, it was corrupt to be impressed by wealth. So I'm corrupt, Allison decided.

"Are your parents still living here?"

"No," Lydia answered. "My mother remarried. She's living in New York also. She married a stock broker. They live on Park Avenue in a very chic building and they do all the right things and go to all the right places and are friends with all the right people and it's all so dull it drives me crazy.

"My own father died when I was two years old," Lydia added. "He was an alcoholic. Drank himself to death."

They had lunch in a small restaurant on the waterfront. Allison was embarrassed when she looked at the menu. The prices were steep and she didn't have enough money on her to pay for her own lunch.

"By the way," Lydia said as if she had been reading her thoughts, "you know this lunch is on me. What about a cocktail first?"

It made her uncomfortable. She didn't think it was right that Lydia pay for her meal. They were just two girl friends dining together and they should have paid for themselves. If not, since Allison had been Lydia's guest for a day and a half, she should have treated Lydia.

Yet, Allison couldn't help admitting to herself that she liked the idea of Lydia's paying for her. It seemed natural somehow. And Allison liked the way Lydia took over in everything else, the way she directed and planned their every move. She even enjoyed riding in Lydia's car. She liked to look at Lydia's hands on the wheel, they were strong, capable looking hands for all their long fingernails and crimson polish.

Coming back to New York, they ran into a traffic jam on the Merritt Parkway. It was getting on toward night and the highway was packed with commuter's cars.

There was a bad accident that tied up traffic ahead of them for almost an hour. Lydia was furious.

"Goddamn it!" she cursed. "This would have to happen just when I'm in a hurry. I've got a date for dinner tonight and afterward I'm meeting a friend for a few drinks. Now I'll barely make it on time for one date before I'll have to leave for the other!"

Allison was disappointed. She had been hoping that Lydia would have dinner with her. "That's too bad," she said. "Maybe we won't be stuck here long."

"And maybe we will. What a rotten bit of luck! Here we are stuck out in the middle of nowhere without even a telephone nearby. Next time I go for a ride with you, I'll remember to bring along a deck of cards so we can play poker.

"I'm blaming you for this, you know. It's all your fault. You've brought me bad luck," Lydia teased.

Allison was stung with hurt. Lydia had been joking, she knew that. Yet, she couldn't help feeling responsible for the accident. She felt guilty even though it was completely illogical.

Allison had always reacted this way. When teachers in school had asked who had been talking or chewing gum or any other misdemeanor, Allison always felt that they were accusing her even if she hadn't been doing anything wrong.

"Tell me about your date," Allison asked to change the topic.

"Paul or Bill? I'm having dinner with Paul and meeting Bill afterward. Which one do you want to hear about?"

"I don't know. Either one. Start with Paul, if you want to."

"Okay," Lydia began. "Paul Spencer, my ex-husband's brother ... which makes him my brother-in-law, I guess. He's in his early forties, married, has two children, a boy and a girl. Paul always likes symmetry.

"His wife is a delightful, charming woman and one of my dearest friends. However, she's a perfect bitch in her own home. She hen-pecks Paul terribly. He's been madly unhappy with her since they married but he didn't know it until I came along.

"Paul has always loved me. He wants to leave his wife for me. Only I don't want him. He's weak. I despise a man who's weak."

"Then why do you bother with him?" Allison asked.

"He amuses me. Besides, he's a damn fine lawyer. He does all my legal work for nothing. All he asks is that I go out to dinner with him occasionally. It's a fair bargain."

"What about Bill?"

"William S. Roman, another old friend. I've known Bill for years. We used to take classes at acting school together.

"You didn't know I used to be an actress, did you? Anyway, I'll tell you all about that another time," Lydia interrupted herself.

"To continue: Bill, as you probably know, is opening in 'Springtime for Annabel' next week. We're getting together tonight to celebrate. It's a tradition with us. Bill says I bring him luck. So we go out before he opens in every new play."

"Is Bill married also?" Allison asked.

"Of course. I wouldn't have anything to do with him if he wasn't."

The logic of this completely escaped Allison. She decided not to explore it at the moment. Maybe she'd be better off not knowing Lydia's reasons for preferring married men.

They could see the two trucks far up ahead on the road coming to tow away the two wrecked cars. It would be several minutes more before the road would be clear again.

"Goddamn it to hell!" Lydia resumed her cursing. "I'm going out of my mind just sitting here. Tell you what, I know a way to pass the time. Open the glove compartment."

Inside the glove compartment there was a silver flask wrapped in leather. Two silver shot glasses were encased in a similar leather cover.

Lydia took the flask from her hand and Allison held the shot glasses while Lydia poured.

"To the state of Connecticut," Lydia raised her glass for a toast. "May it prosper and flourish and may its highway department be cut out of next year's budget."

Allison wasn't used to drinking straight shots. This one didn't even have any ice in it. The liquor burned her throat and made her eyes smart. She managed to get it down by taking small sips.

Lydia downed the contents of her shot glass in one gulp. Immediately, she refilled her glass and downed that one also.

The flask was almost empty by the time they could move again. As soon as the road ahead was clear, Lydia took off like a bat out of hell. She held the gas pedal down to the floor and zigzagged in and out of traffic all the way to Manhattan.

Even so, she was already an hour late for her date by the time they reached Lydia's apartment.

Allison came upstairs with her to help her dress.

As much as she had been in a hurry while they were driving, Lydia took her time about dressing. She selected her outfit for the evening with great care and took an even longer time getting her makeup on just right.

Allison wondered at all this preparation just to meet a couple of "old friends".

Lydia stood up from the vanity table. "Well," she said, "they'll have to be satisfied with the way I look. I can't waste any more time."

Satisfied? Allison thought to herself that Lydia looked gorgeous. She told her so. Lydia looked pleased but she said that Allison was blind in one eye and couldn't see out of the other.

Allison got her coat out of the closet.

"What are you doing with that?" Lydia asked.

"I thought I'd leave when you did."

"What on earth for? Aren't you going to wait here for me?"

"Oh, I couldn't ..."

"Yes you could and will," Lydia interrupted her. "Let's not hear any more about it."

Allison put her coat back in the closet.

"You can keep Prufrock company," Lydia said as she was leaving. "Go to bed if you get tired. I'll wake you up when I come home. I don't know what time I'll be getting in."

She came close to Allison and cupped her chin in her gloved palm. Lydia smiled and brushed her lips against Allison's cheek.

"Be here," she commanded.

CHAPTER FIVE

Allison was dozing lightly when she heard a key turning in the door lock. She sprang to her feet. A quick glance in the mirror confirmed her suspicions, her hair was a mess. No time to do more than run her fingers through it.

Lydia came in looking tired yet exuberant. Her eyes glittered. Her makeup was somewhat worse for wear, her lipstick smeared in one corner.

It didn't matter. It didn't even matter that her chignon had come undone and stray wisps of hair wafted over her ears.

Lydia still looked beautiful.

"Ah," Lydia said when she saw her, "how nice. How indescribably, deliciously nice to come home and find you waiting for me." She pulled her coat off and extended it dramatically. "Take this from me, darling, will you? I don't think I could make it to the closet myself. I'm bushed."

Allison took the coat from her. When she got close, Lydia's breath almost knocked her over. She smelled like a distillery.

Allison took her coat to the closet and hung it up. Meanwhile, Lydia headed for the bedroom, shedding shoes, necklace, earrings and purse on the floor as she walked.

Lydia had her dress off when Allison came into the bedroom. She was struggling to unhook her longline bra.

"Help me, darling. I can't manage this myself."

Allison went around behind Lydia and reached for the hooks. Before she could work on it, Lydia twisted around.

She faced Allison and put her arms around her shoulders. She leaned against her chest. "Do it this way. I want you to hold me up."

Allison felt suffocated. A hot flush rose from her toes up through her body. The nearness of Lydia was driving her mad.

Why was Lydia doing this? She wasn't so drunk she had to be held upright. Was this her idea of being cute? The humor of it escaped Allison.

She reached around and groped for the hooks on Lydia's bra. There were six of them. While she was unhooking them, Lydia inhaled deeply. She buried her head in Allison's hair.

"Um-m-m, you smell good," Lydia said.

The hooks were all loosened. Allison stepped backward, pulling the bra off as she moved.

Lydia's two firm breasts swelled out toward her. Allison tore her eyes away.

She looked at Lydia. Lydia was watching her, her eyes bright and challenging.

It was more than Allison could bear. Hot desire flooded through her. With a low moan, she buried her face in Lydia's breasts, her lips against the soft tips.

She felt Lydia's hand on the top of her head. She circled Lydia in her arms. They fell backward together onto the bed.

"Are you sure, darling?" Lydia asked. "Do you know what you're doing?"

"I don't care."

"But you're so young. No, Allison, you've got to stop this."

Allison stopped her protests with a kiss. She was hungry for Lydia's lips. She caressed and bruised and bit her mouth.

"No … we mustn't …"

Lydia's protests fell on deaf ears. Allison kissed her face, her eyes, her earlobes, the soft hollow of her throat.

Lydia's resistance melted away.

"You bitch," she moaned. "You lovely bitch."

She wrapped her arms tight around Allison and rolled over. Now Allison was lying on the bed with Lydia on top of her. She grabbed the lapel of her bathrobe and ripped it open.

Lydia caressed her breasts. Her palm made slow circles. Allison's breasts were stiff and aching. Then Lydia pressed her body tight against her. Their breasts flattened against each other.

Lydia trailed the tips of her fingers across Allison's throbbing thighs.

"Oh, yes, yes."

Lydia's mouth was on her breast. She flicked her tongue around and around … maddeningly. Her fingertips evoked aching paths of fire on Allison's thighs.

She grabbed Lydia's hand.

Lydia allowed her to direct her hand for a moment. Then she tore it away.

She bit Allison's breast sharply. Then raised herself up and moved toward the foot of the bed, her lips trailing down Allison's body.

Allison gasped. Her head reeled with the sudden shock of contact. She arched her back.

Rockets of pleasure went off inside her. She was dazzled, overwhelmed. Straining muscles pulled against each other. Bursts of perfect joy filled her.

Allison let go. She fell back onto the bed, limp and exhausted.

She felt so warm and blissful. For a long while Allison listened silently to the beating of her own heart.

Lydia pulled herself up and lay alongside Allison. She kissed Allison gently, her passion was spent.

The next day Lydia told Allison she wanted her to live with her. She outlined the way it would work.

Allison wouldn't have to work any more. Lydia could support both of them. Her only responsibility would be to be available to Lydia as a loving companion.

They drove to Allison's apartment that afternoon and packed her clothes. It wasn't until she was already unpacking her bags in her new home that Allison realized she had had no say in the matter. She had never even so much as told Lydia she wanted to live with her.

Lydia had taken that for granted. And she had taken it for granted that Allison would allow herself to be kept.

Would she?

Indeed she would. It was evidence of Lydia's feeling for her that she wanted to support her. Besides, Allison felt the same way she did. Her main reason for not wanting to get a job was that it would mean so many hours away from Lydia.

It all seemed very lovely at first. And later, as Allison learned more and more about Lydia, it was ugly and horrible.

Yet she stayed on and endured it all. Because it was necessary—because she couldn't live without Lydia—because she loved her.

She was Lydia's kept woman. It didn't matter a bit that they were both females. She was Lydia's private whore as much as she could be any man's.

Lydia kept two pets, the Doberman and Allison. Prufrock guarded Lydia against housebreakers and Allison performed her tour of duty in bed. Also, she had to follow Lydia everywhere as if she, too, were on a leash.

Lydia dominated her completely. That's the way Lydia liked it, the way she insisted it be. And deep down, Allison liked it that way too.

But why not try to find someone else? Someone who would be kinder to her. If Lydia went for her, other women probably would too. She could attract a man even more easily. No, that was out. Allison didn't want a man to touch her ever again. Like it or not, she had to accept that she was a lesbian.

Then what about another woman? There were loads of well-to-do women, aging dykes who were looking for pretty girls. So what if they wouldn't be as beautiful as Lydia or as stimulating or as heavenly in bed? What difference would that make? At least someone else would treat her better than Lydia did. She wouldn't have to face all the humiliation and torture with someone else.

So why continue putting up with a sickminded, sadistic bitch like Lydia Stone?

Why?

Because she loved her.

In the months they lived together Allison learned a lot about Lydia's strange needs. She had never even suspected that anyone practiced some of the things Lydia went in for.

She had tried to get away once. A couple of months after they had been living together, Allison decided she just couldn't take it any longer. She had to get away before the last shreds of human dignity were destroyed within her.

She wrote a note explaining everything to Lydia and left it for her when Lydia was busy on the telephone talking to Bill one afternoon. She slipped quietly out of the apartment and was down the stairs and out of the building as fast as she could run.

It was fine and glorious to be free. She felt like singing as she walked through the snowy streets.

The headache began when she reached the corner of Greenwich Avenue and Sixth Avenue. It had been so long since she had had an attack—ever since meeting Lydia—that Allison couldn't really believe this one would develop into anything bad.

She continued walking south on Sixth Avenue. The pain mounted, throbbing dully at the base of her skull. She felt weak and dizzy. Halos of colored lights appeared around everything.

She was standing in front of the Waverly Theatre, trying to focus her eyes so she could read what was playing on the marquee, when the sun came out from behind a cloud.

The sunlight glittered off the banks of snow piled at the curb. Allison felt the brilliant sparkle sear into her brain.

She fell to the sidewalk.

When she came to there was a small crowd of people around her. A policeman came rushing up. He asked her if she wanted him to call an ambulance.

No, she didn't need to go to a hospital. What good would that do? She knew why the headache had come on and what would cure it. And no doctor could prescribe Lydia pills.

The policeman offered to see her safely home.

Allison hesitated for a moment. Where should she tell him she lived? What was the use? She'd be going back there soon anyway. She gave him Lydia's address.

The policeman insisted on seeing her all the way upstairs. He waited with her until Lydia opened the door. Then he came inside with them and told Lydia all about what had happened.

After the policeman left, Allison felt a moment of acute fear. She should never have come back. She would have been better off dead than here.

It was no use even thinking about it. She had had to come back. It was the ultimate surrender to Lydia's domination and she had made it.

Allison felt completely submissive. Like a child, she was stripped of all adult willpower. She was helpless as she had been as a child when her mother had lashed her with endless nagging criticisms.

"Do you know why you got sick?" Lydia interrupted her thoughts.

"Yes, I know."

"Tell me about it."

Allison began in a dead voice. "It was because I need you and I can't stand to be away from you."

"True enough. But you're being selfish, as usual. You're not thinking of what you did to me. I was worried, Allison. Your note upset me very much. I didn't know where you were, what was happening to you."

"I'm sorry. It was wrong of me."

"Yes, very wrong. You've always been a bad girl, haven't you, Allison? Even when you were a child?"

"Yes."

"What makes you be so bad all the time?"

"I don't know."

Lydia's eyes glinted with a steel-blue light. "You're not going to be bad anymore, are you, Allison? Promise me that. Remember that I support you completely. Everything you have comes from me. And so I expect you to obey me."

Allison nodded. Her head still throbbed. She would give anything to make the pain go away.

"You're never going to be unkind to me again. That's right, isn't it, Allison?"

"Yes. I'll try very hard to be everything you want me to be."

"I've been treating you too gently," Lydia went on. "From now on I'm going to punish you every time you're bad."

"Please, Lydia, don't lecture me anymore. Anything you say is all right with me but please stop nagging me."

"But I've got to punish you so you'll never run away again. Did your mother ever punish you any other way? Did she ever spank you, Allison?"

Allison told her about the time when she had been a little girl. She told her about seeing her mother and father in bed together and about the way her mother had beaten her. Lydia listened eagerly, her mouth trembling with excitement.

"That seems to have made a lasting impression on you," Lydia said when she was finished. "Perhaps you need some of the same again. Would you like me to spank you?"

Allison didn't answer. She stared dumbly at the floor.

"Look at me and answer me, Allison. You were bad, just like you were as a little girl. Don't you agree that you should be spanked?"

Anything, anything to stop this agonizing interrogation. "Yes," she mumbled.

"Take your clothes off."

Allison obeyed silently. She could feel Lydia's eyes on her as she undressed. She stood naked in front of Lydia. Lydia's eyes moved slowly from the peaks of her beautiful breasts down to her most intimate areas.

"Walk," Lydia commanded. "Walk back and forth in front of me."

Allison walked, feeling Lydia's eyes on every line and curve of her body.

"Now, come with me."

Obediently, Allison followed her into the bedroom.

Lydia took her clothes off and sat down on the edge of the bed. She motioned for Allison to lie across her knees.

"Remember, this is because you deserve to be punished. Just like when you were a little girl and your mother punished you because you were bad."

Lydia's breath came in shallow gasps. She slapped Allison with the palms of her hands, showering blows with one hand after the other on her tender backside.

The spanking grew in intensity. Lydia slapped harder and harder.

"You're hurting me," Allison protested.

"Of course, I'm punishing you."

The pain was too much. Great tears formed in the corners of her eyes and rolled down Allison's cheeks. She began to sob softly.

Lydia stopped spanking her. She lifted her up and eased her gently down on the bed.

"Why are you crying?"

"You hurt me," Allison replied.

"Did your mother hurt you when she spanked you?"

"Yes. You—you hurt me just like my mother did."

"Allison, Allison, my poor baby." She wrapped her arms around her and rocked gently. Lydia kissed the path the tears had followed on her cheeks.

"I love you so very much," Allison murmured.

Lydia gasped. Her body trembled with desire. She made love to Allison, kissing every inch of her body ... especially the sore part where her palms had raised red welts.

After that afternoon, Allison never disobeyed Lydia again. She suffered everything in silence. No matter how low Lydia made her sink, Allison put up with it. All trace of decency had gone out of her life.

Lydia made her take a lot. Things like the truth about her association with Bill and other men.

They were Lydia's lovers. Lydia liked making love to a girl but she couldn't stand to have a girl touch her intimately. She said it revolted her. She wanted a man when she was on her back.

Lydia brought her lovers to the apartment. She made Allison cook dinner for them and be polite to them even though she knew that Allison hated their guts. And after dinner, when the real entertainment of the evening began, she made Allison come into the bedroom with them and watch while the men made love to her.

Sometimes she took Allison to a gay bar in the Village. Lydia picked up girls in the bar—sometimes two or three—and brought them home. They had wild orgies. Lydia liked to have Allison watch her making love to another woman. She taunted her that she wasn't as good a lover as the other woman had been.

Then Lydia had hit on the idea of making Allison go to bed with men for money. She knew that Allison hated being touched by a man. The issue of money made it even more humiliating.

They didn't need the money. That wasn't the issue. The money angle was for kicks. Besides, Lydia enjoyed watching Allison squirm while she haggled with a customer.

Allison grew to hate Lydia. And she loved her at the same time. She needed Lydia. Everything about her that was mean and cruel excited Allison, made her desire Lydia more.

More than she hated Lydia, she hated herself.

She hated herself because she was sick and rotten inside and she couldn't break away from the sordid mess she had gotten herself into.

She was no good inside, evil. Evil should be punished.

And Lydia punished her.

CHAPTER SIX

Time to get up.

Allison watched the rim of light shining around the edges of the drawn window blind grow gradually brighter. Soon Lydia would be awake.

She slipped gingerly out of bed.

No hangover this morning. That was an improvement. But she felt stiff and dragged out from lack of sleep.

How long had she lain awake last night? Christ, it must have been hours. And all those horrible memories. Better not to think about them.

She could control her thoughts during the daytime usually. Come night and her mind seemed to have a will of its own. Then, if she lay awake wracked and tortured by horrible memories, she could only wait for them to go on until blessed sleep released her.

Lydia was still sleeping.

She looked lovely. Pink and gold against the white background of the sheets. She was deeply asleep, her knees drawn up, her arms around the pillow.

Lydia always looked her best when she was asleep. Relaxed, the defiant expression in her eyes and around her mouth softened. She looked feminine and soft and vulnerable.

It was a wonder that Lydia was still so beautiful. She admitted to being thirty-five and Allison privately thought she was at least three or four years older. Lydia had lived every moment of her life to the fullest. Yet she didn't show any signs of aging. Her body was firm, her skin smooth and lovely.

How could a woman look so innocent and beautiful and be so cruel?

It didn't make sense. Not much did to Allison any more. Things worked out for her somehow though. She just followed along behind Lydia, accepting everything that came her way and life went on.

The shower took some of the ache out of her bones. She came out of the shower and towelled herself dry briskly. She felt almost happy. Not quite but almost.

She could never be completely happy as long as she lived with Lydia.

The doorbell rang.

Allison called, "I'll get it," and, throwing a terrycloth bathrobe on, ran to the door.

It was the deliveryman from the dry cleaning store delivering Lydia's black silk cocktail dress.

Allison took the dress from him and hung it in the closet. She wondered idly why Lydia had had it cleaned. Then she remembered.

This was the day of Bill's party.

"Who was that?" Lydia asked from the bedroom.

"The cleaner's. They brought your dress back," Allison replied as she walked back into the bedroom.

Lydia was sitting up in bed. She never wore anything to bed even in the dead of winter. The lower part of her body was hidden under the sheet.

Allison looked at her. Lydia's breasts were magnificent. They were full and lush and soft. In spite of her thirty-five or more years, Lydia's breasts were firm. They pointed out toward Allison invitingly. Touch me, the breasts seemed to be saying.

Allison ran to the bed and knelt beside it. She buried her face in the cleft between Lydia's breasts.

It was so warm there, so peaceful. She inhaled the mixture of perfume and musky body odor which was Lydia's special odor.

"I love you," Allison said.

Lydia put her hand on the back of her neck and pressed her face against her chest. The sheet slipped down, revealing her body down to the middle of her thighs.

Allison felt the familiar heat reddening her cheeks. She wanted to touch Lydia. To take her face out of the cleft and put her mouth on Lydia's breast. She wanted to run her hands all over the silken loveliness of Lydia's body.

But she couldn't. She had to force herself to think about other things and forget about the lovely body so near.

She couldn't because Lydia wouldn't let her. Because Lydia called herself an "untouchable butch" and that meant she didn't like having a woman make love to her. She got her kicks from making the other woman sweat and writhe.

It was true. Allison had seen it happen. She had seen the way Lydia reacted when they were making love. Lydia got just as worked up as Allison. Sometimes more. She liked to watch Lydia when the tension was building up to the bursting point. Lydia came right along with her all the way.

Only that wasn't enough for Lydia. She liked to be made love to also. Only it had to be a man. She said that the two kinds of love-making were completely different for her. The kicks she got with a man were different from the way she felt with a woman. It was the other side of the coin for her. Lydia liked a man to abuse her in bed. Even though she was a controlling bitch with everyone in every other sort of situation, in bed with a man Lydia liked him to act as if he were her master.

Allison had watched her make love that way lots of times. It looked ridiculous. The men only slapped and whipped Lydia because she wanted them to. They weren't forcing her, she was the one who was controlling everything.

Even though Lydia was no longer an actress her interest in theatre remained. Only now she played the director. It came out clearly when she was having sex.

"We made ourselves $125 last night," Lydia reminded her.

Allison winced. She wished they could just act as if it had never happened.

"What should I wear tonight?" she asked to change the topic.

"Um…let's see," Lydia frowned in concentration. "What about those new black velvet skinny pants and a white silk blouse?"

"To the party?"

"Sure. Bill's parties are informal. There will be lots of girls there in slacks."

"But I thought you were going to wear your black formal."

"I am. So?"

"Well, won't we look kind of funny coming in together if I'm in pants and you're all dressed up? I mean, don't you think that's advertising ourselves a bit too much?"

"What's wrong with that?" Lydia grinned. "Don't you want people to know you're my woman?"

Lydia's sense of the absolutely perfect thing to say was infallible. Allison had no more objections. So many people, men and women, found Lydia desirable. Allison loved seeing them envy her when they found out she was Lydia's lover.

"What kind of a party is this going to be, anyway?"

"Oh, I'd forgotten that you've never been to one of Bill's parties before," Lydia answered. "Well, they're all pretty much the same."

"And what's that?"

"Far out, baby, real far out. Bill collects all the weirdies in New York and turns them loose on each other."

"It doesn't sound like the sort of thing you usually go in for."

Lydia laughed. "On the contrary. You'll see. It takes a little while for everybody to relax, but after they've had some drinks and some other choice goodies Bill keeps for these occasions, it gets to be just exactly what I go for."

Allison felt an icy hand gripping her heart. "How so?"

"One never knows. Not in advance. All I can tell you is, if you dig anything, anything at all on earth, you'll find it at Bill's parties."

The party was just beginning when they arrived. People kept arriving every few minutes, singly and in couples. Soon the posh apartment was jammed. It was quite an assortment. There were men there who looked and dressed like out of work folksingers and others who were obviously professors of Archaeology. There were women in jeans and sweatshirts, others decked out in glittering finery who were actresses and others who looked like, talked like, and undoubtedly were ladies of negotiable virtue.

Lydia was making with the flirty-flirty bit with some character in baggy tweeds and an unlighted briar pipe. Strictly Klein's basement stuff left out in the rain deliberately to get that "casual" look.

Allison took her cue. Lydia didn't want her around. She was going to make out with the men that night. Naturally, it was too good an opportunity for her to pass up. She could maybe meet something good and drive both Allison and Bill out of their minds with jealousy at the same time.

Allison looked around for someone to talk to. Lydia would want her to make like she was enjoying herself. That was the way Lydia always liked her to act. She knew damn well that Allison didn't like watching her turn on the charm toward other people and she knew that Allison couldn't be less interested in making out with a man herself. That didn't matter. Lydia insisted that she suffer inwardly only.

There were a few people in the place whom Allison had met before. One of them, Jim Harrington, was sitting alone, looking unhappy.

She started walking toward him. At least he'd be someone to talk to while she drank her first Sidecar. Jim was a bore. More than that, he was a reliable bore. You could always count on him to tell you all about his psychoanalysis in great detail as if he were the first human being to have gotten a swift kick in the psyche. Oh well, at least he had such a strong transference toward his analyst that he wouldn't want to make a pass at her until he was thoroughly drunk.

Someone grabbed her elbow. She turned. An incredibly thin, blonde man with a scraggly beard was holding her.

"Calvin Staton," he introduced himself, "boy abstract realist."

"And I'm the Duchess of Alba," Allison retorted, twisting out of his grip.

"Bad bit," he criticized, grabbing her arm again. "You're more the Modigliani type. You reek of suffering spirituality."

"Yes!" A fat girl in a turtle-necked sweater who had been sitting on the floor next to them jumped to her feet and joined in. "You're right. I can see it all. She'll do great things and then one day drown herself in the ocean, leaving a note to her husband telling him never to eat shellfish."

It was amusing. Yet, Allison couldn't help feeling contemptuous. All of these people with their high I.Qs. and they could find nothing better to do with themselves than fling mangled literary references around at each other. So much potential talent going to waste. So much reading just so they would have things to talk to each other about.

"Do you always stand in third position?" the man named Calvin asked.

She looked down at her feet. He was right. She was in third position.

"I always stand this way because it's comfortable," she told him.

"Nonsense," he sneered. "You're like everyone else. You're dependent on the opinion of others for your own sense of identity.

And you stand that way because you want me to think you're a dancer."

"I'm not a dancer..."

"Of course not. You're a lyric poet. I could tell the minute I saw you," the fat girl crowed.

Allison ignored her completely and went back to telling the bearded man off. "Furthermore, I don't like being categorized. You could at least have the courtesy to save your little analysis of my personality until you got to know me better."

"Courtesy!" he said it as if it were a dirty word. "Courtesy is the opiate of the bourgeoise."

She disliked him intensely. He was phony and pretentious and rude.

And he was being even more rude now. His cold blue eyes were looking her over carefully. Boldly he stared at the place where the low neckline of her blouse revealed the rounded swell of her bosom.

He was good-looking though. If you looked past the paint-smeared dungarees and the torn lumber shirt and imagined him without the beatnik stubble on his chin, Calvin Staton was very handsome.

He just kept staring at her, his hard blue eyes expressionless. Allison found her repugnance melting away. No wonder he was so self-confident. A good-looking guy like him probably didn't have any trouble getting women.

She wondered what it would be like to be with him. How would it feel to have his arms around her?

It had been so long since she had even kissed a man except when Lydia was there directing the whole thing. That was an entirely different thing. Now Allison wondered what it would be like to be alone with Calvin Staton. What it would be like to be dominated by a man instead of a woman.

Sure, Lydia satisfied her in bed. She didn't have to look else-where for sexual gratification. Yet, after the newness of their relationship had worn off and the months had gone by, Allison sensed something was wrong. Making love with Lydia was wonderful. It never failed to leave her drained of all tension, relaxed and glowing. And yet, there had been a gnawing sense of something missing. She didn't know what to call it but she did know that afterward, while she was listening to the soft sound of Lydia breathing deeply beside her, Allison felt hungry for something more.

Lydia needed men. Maybe this was the missing element that would make the equation complete. Allison wondered if she too would feel satisfied if she let a man make love to her. Not a brutal beast like Steve Callum had been. Maybe she would feel all she was supposed to feel with an artist, a sensitive man like Calvin Staton.

She wanted to find out. Right now. She wanted to fling herself at him and have him take her before she had time to think about anything else.

It frightened her to think about such a thing. She took a long pull on her drink and looked away from him while she collected her thoughts.

Jim Harrington slouched over. Not bothering to greet her, he began, "I think I ought to change analysts. Does anyone here know of a good one."

Allison shook her head.

"What about you?" Jim asked Calvin.

"Don't believe in analysis."

"What?!!!" Jim sounded as shocked as if he had just been told that Marilyn Monroe was really Arthur Miller in drag.

"Nope. Lot of crap," Calvin went on.

"But what do you do about your complexes, and obsessions and ..."

Calvin leaned close to Jim. Dropping his voice to a deep, solemn tone he said, "I swing, man. You know, like making it. Like life is going on all around you and you're lying on a goddamned couch telling this jerk all about how your mother caught you masturbating when you were eight years old. Like, man, that's not the way to do it. Like you got to roll with it. Swing, ya know what I mean?" Jim looked like he didn't understand a word. He looked at Allison for an explanation.

She shook her head helplessly. Jim was a big enough fool all by himself. Calvin had reduced him to a figure of absolute absurdity.

"I know of a very good analyst," the earnest fat girl broke in. "He's a Jungian. He'll tell you how all the things you dream about really come from ancestral memories..." She put her hand on Jim's arm and the two of them sank to the floor, she babbling on at a furious pace and Jim listening with complete absorption.

"Your glass is empty, Duchess."

For a moment she couldn't remember why he called her that. Then she giggled self-consciously. "My name is Allison. Allison Fuller."

"All right, Allison Fuller, you need a fresh drink."

She held the glass out. He didn't make a move, even to taking the glass from her.

Calvin's eyes darkened with anger. "What do you expect me to do? Get your drink for you? You crippled or something? Goddamned women always hollering about a single standard and then you expect the men to play Sir Galahad."

"All right, I'll get it for myself. And please don't shout at me. I just thought you wanted to get a drink for me."

"Why should I want to?"

"Because that's the way men like to act with women."

"Crap," Calvin answered succinctly. "The way a man likes to act with a woman is what he does to her in bed. Anything else is just a way of getting her to drop her pants."

"That's so true." An effeminate little man wearing thick horn-rimmed glasses joined her. "That, I believe, is one of the great truisms of life. I think I'll write a book about it." He hiccouped loudly and downed half the contents of a highball glass in one swallow.

"My analyst says that every woman I go to bed with is just a substitute for my mother," Jim offered from the floor where he was sitting.

"How very interesting," the effeminate man squealed. He sat down next to Jim on the floor. "Tell me more about it. How did you feel about your Father?"

"I'm going to the john. You want to come with me?" Cal said.

She looked at him as if he were insane. "W-what?"

"Come to the john with me," Calvin repeated slowly, as if he were talking to a child. "I got to take a leak. What's the matter? Haven't you ever seen a man with his fly open before?"

"I'm going to the bar to get another drink," Allison said hastily. "I—I'll see you when you come back."

"Your loss," Calvin said as he turned and strode away.

Lydia was standing next to the bar talking to Bill and another couple. She put her arm around Allison's shoulder and hugged her.

"Having fun, honey?"

"Sure. Lots of real weirdies here, though."

"You'll get used to them," Bill said. "Here, this will help put you in the right mood." He dropped a thin cigarette into Allison's hand.

"Be right back. Got to make sure everyone's taken care of." Bill went around the room organizing his guests into groups of about ten. He gave two of the thin cigarettes to each group.

There were eight people in their group. Allison looked around for Calvin. She saw him sitting on the floor, already lighting one of the cigarettes.

"I got a fresh batch this week," Bill informed them. "Good stuff. Straight from Mexico. I rolled them this afternoon. Hope I made enough. I only rolled sixty of them and there are thirty people here. But it's good strong stuff. I know. I tried it and, man, I went straight out of my mind before I had finished the first one."

"It's enough. If not, we'll roll some more. Knock everybody on his ass," a white-haired woman who looked like a Cub Scout denmother said.

Bill pulled up a hassock for Lydia to sit on. The rest of them just sat in a circle on the floor. Bill leaned against the hassock on one side and Allison inclined her shoulder against Lydia's thigh on the other side.

A little bubble of fear rose up in Allison's throat. This had never happened before. It wasn't the first time she had tried marijuana. A couple of times before she had taken a few puffs at a party. Just enough to feel a pleasant warmth and relaxation.

This time was going to be different because Lydia was joining in. She usually didn't. Lydia generally preferred to stick to liquor. Allison had suffered plenty the times when too much booze had brought out the violent side of Lydia's sadism. She didn't know whether the marijuana would have the same effect or something worse.

There was another angle to it. Lydia would want her to match her puff for puff. This time, Allison would get really high. It frightened her not to know what her own reaction would be.

The other members of the group watched hungrily while Bill lit up the first *joint*. He had a little trouble getting it started. The cigarettes were clumsily made, the paper wrapper twisted into a hard knot at the ends to keep the contents from spilling out. The twisted paper flared up in a burst of flame then went out.

Bill cursed and lit another match. He held it to the end of the joint until it was properly burning. Then he took a big drag, opened his mouth and sucked in and swallowed a gulp of air along with the smoke. That would get him high faster than just inhaling ordinarily.

Bill held his lips tightly closed, not breathing. The longer he could hold the smoke down in his lungs, the more effective it would be. He passed the joint on to Lydia.

Allison watched her. Lydia turned on like a pro. No doubting it, she was an old hand with *pot*.

Then it was Allison's turn. She imitated the way Bill and Lydia had inhaled. She got a big gulp of air and smoke into her mouth then swallowed it. It tasted good, richer than an ordinary cigarette. But the smoke scorched her throat as it went down. She fought to keep herself from exhaling it too soon, the effort and the raw burning in her throat making her eyes water.

She passed the joint to the matronly-looking woman who was sitting next to her. By passing it around they were able to get the most out of it before it burned down.

Bill leaned over and offered Allison a sip of Scotch from his glass. She needed it. Even the raw liquor was soothing to her parched throat.

Bill took back the cigarette he had given her before. The first one was going from the fourth to the fifth person in the group.

Bill lit the second joint and started that one on the rounds of the group. With two of them going, there was just time to breathe before taking another puff.

The second puff was easier to take. Allison took in a lot of air this time and it seemed to cool the smoke. Her throat didn't burn as badly.

When the smoke hit her lungs, something seemed to burst inside her. It was hitting her. Her body felt loose and weightless. Her senses became more acute.

She closed her eyes. How nice to feel her body and yet not quite feel it. It was almost as it were someone else's body she was examining. She could imagine what it looked like inside, all full of miraculous little twisty things that worked together in blissful compatibility.

The cigarettes were burned down so far they burned the fingers of the person who was holding them. Bill ripped the covers off two matchbooks. He rolled them around the ends of the cigarettes and, using the matchbooks as holders, the group smoked the *roaches* down until there were only a couple of grains of marijuana left at the very end.

Through a glass wall that somehow made everything brighter and clearer than normal, Allison watched the white-haired woman pinch the ends of the matchbooks together to put out the cigarettes. Then she carefully extracted the eighth of an inch of cigarette that was left, put it in her mouth and washed it down with a big drink.

That was a new one. Allison wondered idly what the idea was. Did it have some special kind of effect if you ate it? Must taste ghastly.

I'm high, Allison thought to herself. She sat on the floor and thought about how very high she was indeed.

It was wonderful. She felt great. No problems, no worries. Peace. For the first time, really. She could never remember having felt this way before. Even as a child she had been anxious all the time, afraid of something or somebody.

Now, nothing mattered. Not tomorrow nor yesterday. Even Lydia didn't matter. To hell with her and her nastiness.

There was a lot of noise coming from one end of the large room. About twenty men and women were playing stripping games. They giggled like little children as they took their clothes off. The women were better sports, they took all their clothes off. Some of them looked silly, standing around naked with their makeup and jewelry still on.

The men were shyer. All except two of them kept their shoes and socks and shorts on.

They looked funny. Allison laughed.

She pulled herself slowly to her feet. The room rocked for a moment and it seemed to take her a long time before she was erect.

The little game in the corner was spreading throughout the room. Almost everyone was at least half-undressed.

Allison felt someone unbuttoning her blouse. It was Lydia. She was smiling strangely, her mouth pulled up crookedly.

"Come on, get out of these things and join the party."

Allison stood perfectly still while Lydia undressed her. Some man she had never seen before was helping.

When she was naked, the man stood in back of her and cupped her breasts in his hands.

Allison tore herself out of his grasp.

Lydia stood with her eyes closed, swaying gently. It was as if she were listening to some inner melody.

Allison groped for her. The silken skin felt more delicious than it ever had before.

Lydia gasped. She flung her head back; a low moan came from far back in her throat.

She was going crazy. She could hardly breathe. Sounds like sobbing tore from her throat.

"Wonderful," Lydia breathed. "I—" she opened her eyes.

"Allison! What the hell ..."

She tore herself away and stood up. "You know I don't go for that bit," she said and walked away, looking for a man.

Allison followed her. She didn't know why. It didn't really matter that Lydia wouldn't let her make love to her.

Nothing mattered very much.

Following Lydia was just something to do.

The woman with the white hair, who looked like an ad for baking powder biscuits, walked over to where two young men were talking together. One of them was sitting on a chair, the other was sitting on the floor looking up at him adoringly.

The woman sat down on the lap of the one in the chair. She ran her fingers through his hair and told him how handsome and strong he was.

The boy on the floor snorted in disgust and looked away.

"What's the matter with him?" she asked.

"He's just jealous. Aren't you, Davey?"

The boy on the floor looked as if he were going to cry. "How can you let her touch you that way?" he asked with a pronounced lisp.

"Didn't I tell you, Davey? I like an occasional dose of the other."

The woman was annoyed because they weren't paying enough attention to her. She stood up and grabbed the hand of the boy in the chair. "Wouldn't you like to go into another room with me where we could have more privacy?"

The boy grinned and looked down at his companion. "What about it, Davey? Care to join us?"

"No, thank you very much anyway."

"Come on, I'll show you something I'll bet you've never tried before."

"But she's a *girl!*" Davey protested.

"Never mind that. I guarantee you'll like what we're going to do." He linked his arms through those of Davey and the woman. "Like to make a sandwich, mother?"

"I don't care what we do. Just let's hurry!" she said.

They left the room.

Jim Harrington and the fat girl walked down the long hall hand in hand. They tried every door. Most of them were locked. The others, the unlocked rooms, were very much occupied. There was nowhere in the whole apartment where they could be alone.

Jim shook his head mournfully. "This is awful. My analyst told me I should have more relations with women. He says I'm too inhibited."

"That's bad. You shouldn't be inhibited."

"But what are we going to do? Every bed in the place is in use."

"You should do what your analyst tells you to do," the fat girl said.

"I know. And I really do want to have sex tonight. I'm in the mood for it."

"Me too."

"But we can't just do it out here in the hall."

"Why not?" she asked.

"Someone might come by. They might see us."

"You're afraid because you're inhibited. You should fight your inhibitions."

"Think so?" he asked.

"Yes."

"That's what my analyst says too."

They dropped to the floor.

Calvin Staton was looking for the lovely black-haired girl he had been talking to earlier in the evening.

He couldn't seem to find her in the crowd.

Once he thought he saw her walking across the room. He ran after her but she disappeared through a door before he could reach her.

When he got to the place where she had been, he saw that what he had taken for a door was actually a window.

Must be the pot. Man, I must be real stoned if I can't tell a door from a window, he reflected. Better take it easy with some juice.

He walked across the room to the bar. His feet seemed a million miles away from his body.

Allison walked six paces behind Lydia and the man she was with. They went down the long hall, looking for an unoccupied room.

A boy and a girl were tangled together in front of one of the doors. Lydia and the man stepped over them and opened the door. The room was empty. They entered and closed the door behind them.

Allison followed.

She moved with great effort, having to concentrate on lifting her feet.

As she stepped over the couple, the boy looked up.

"Hi," Jim said.

"Hi. Hope I'm not disturbing you."

"Not at all," the fat girl answered for them both.

"I'm glad," Allison said.

She turned the knob. Nothing happened. The door was locked from the inside. She knocked.

"Who is it?"

"Me, Allison."

"What do you want?"

"I want to come in."

"Allison, go away," Lydia called out.

"Go away where?"

"Anywhere. Just leave us alone."

"I haven't got anything to do."

"Go out to the living room and find somebody to talk to," Lydia said.

"I don't want to talk to anybody."

"Then for Christ's sake, go and get yourself laid! Only get the hell away from here."

The tall woman with the champagne colored hair closed in on him slowly. She was talking to another man and her back was turned on Calvin.

That didn't stop her. She knew where she was heading and how to get there. She took a step backward and then paused a long while before taking another. Her companion didn't even notice her movement.

Calvin watched her with amusement. He tried to estimate how long it would take her to get where she was going. He waited without any particular sensation beyond curiosity.

She was directly in front of him now. Her spike-heeled shoes touching the sides of his.

It took limber muscles to accomplish what she was doing. Cal was impressed.

Still facing the other man and carrying on an animated conversation with him, the woman had thrown her spine all out of alignment. The twin cantaloupes of her buttocks swung uncertainly from side to side for a moment and then she found her goal.

Cal stood still and let her play her little game. Christ, she had a behind! There was no end to the variations in pressure she could work with it.

She leaned her whole body up against him.

Ignoring the man she had been talking to, she turned her head so that her mouth was close to Calvin's ear.

"Want to make it with me?" she asked.

"This way?"

"Any way. You name it."

"I don't know, I'm pretty knocked out," he teased.

"You won't have to work hard. Leave it to me." She ran the tip of her tongue over the outline of her lips suggestively.

"Um-m-m, that's an idea. What about something else?"

"I told you, anything else."

"Even if it hurts?"

"What's a little pain between friends?"

"Crazy! Come on, let's go somewhere where we can be alone." He took her arm and guided her away from the bar.

The man she had been talking to went on speaking even though no one was listening to him.

Calvin slid his hand off her arm and ran it over her buttocks as they walked through the crowded room. "I like a girl who doesn't mind a little pain between friends," he said.

"My name is Margo. What's yours?" the woman asked.

Allison sat on the floor in a corner of the big room. It seemed to her that she was actually in the center of the room and all the people were surrounding her on all sides.

Nobody spoke to her. She was all alone.

That was all right. That was the way it should be. She wasn't lonely. She was just waiting.

For what?

For something to happen.

Allison tried to think of what she would like to happen.

She couldn't think of anything.

It didn't matter. Lydia would be along soon and she would tell her what to do.

Lydia was having a fine time. God, this pot was great! Even better than booze.

Too bad the guy turned out to be a dud. She looked at him lying on the rumpled bed beside her, his eyes closed.

Oh, he had been o.k. for a while. Very o.k. as a matter of fact.

But what good was he now?

Too bad. He had been a good one.

Lydia rubbed her palms down her sides and smiled as she remembered.

Wow! What a ball it had been! It had seemed to last for hours, building up slowly.

What a kick! This pot really had something to it.

She wondered if Bill had any more. It would be interesting to see what would happen if she smoked another one.

Where the hell was Bill, anyway?

Lydia frowned in annoyance. He had a hell of a nerve, just disappearing like that. The least he could have done was act a little jealous when she went off with another man.

Lydia got out of the bed. She was going to go find Bill and maybe smoke another *stick* while she gave him a piece of her mind.

✤ ✤ ✤

Calvin Staton sat up on the bed. He felt crummy. If he could figure out where his clothes were, he'd put them on and get out of
this joint.

His high was almost all gone. Balling that blonde chick had
knocked it out of him. Now he felt sober and disgusted.

Jesus, what a whore that one had been; Disgusting. The noises
she made! Like a hog rooting in a trough.

How could he have done it? Come off it, boy, he told himself.
You've done it before and with worse pigs than this one.

Why?

Because, man, you got to have a lot of it and when you haven't
got a chick of your own, you make it with whatever broad is
available.

He felt dirty. A shower would feel good.

Dimly, he remembered that there had been a bathroom at the
end of the hall.

The door to the bathroom was open a crack. Just to make
sure no one was using it, Calvin knocked on the bathroom
door.

There was no answer.

He opened the door.

Two men were in there. They were too busy with what they
were doing to notice him.

Finally, one of them looked up and saw Calvin standing in
the doorway. "We've got company, love," he told the other man.

The guy turned around. "Say now, where did this lovely
number come from? He's a handsome one, isn't he, sugar?"

"Divine, simply divine. Care to join us, handsome?"

"Go get yourself a duck," Calvin sneered. He banged the
bathroom door shut behind him.

Better to get his clothes on and get out of here. What a cess-
pool this place was.

That girl with the black hair and green eyes had been nice. Not like the other cruds at the party.

Hard to tell in this atmosphere, though. No doubt about the fact that she wasn't completely right in the head. Maybe not too bad. Maybe it was just something she could get over.

Lydia and Bill were sharing a joint between them. Allison sat beside Lydia, her face expressionless.

"Dig this stuff?" Bill asked.

"The end. Makes me want to keep going all night," Lydia answered.

"That's nothing new for you," Bill grinned. "You ready to go it again with me?"

"Yes. But not here."

"Why not?"

"I don't know. It's just that it's sort of phony around here. All these young kids banging each other. Makes me kind of sad. I want to go where they do it for real. Bill, let's go Valerie's."

"All the way up to Harlem at this hour?"

"Sure. Come on, Valerie will give us a room."

"Why do we have to go there? We can make it right here, in my own place."

"You know I get excited at Valerie's, Bill. It kicks me to shack up in a whore house."

"Aw, hell, I don't feel like going all the way up there."

"You want to feel me, Bill?"

"You know I always want that, baby."

"Then let's go to Valerie's."

Allison spoke up for the first time as they started to walk away from her. "Hey," she called, "what about me? I want to go too."

"I don't want you," Lydia said. "Can't you find something to do by yourself?"

"No," Allison pouted. "I don't like it here. I want to go home."

"Then go home."

"Here," Bill pushed a five-dollar bill into her hand. "Take a cab home and sleep it off. You'll feel better in the morning."

"I don't want to go home alone. I'll wait here until Lydia comes back from Valerie's."

"I'll be going straight home from Valerie's and you goddamn well better be there when I get home," Lydia said.

"When will that be?"

"How do I know? Sometime tomorrow, I guess."

"But what should I do until then?" Allison wailed.

"Get yourself laid, baby. You've got my blessings." Lydia turned on her heel and walked away with Bill.

Allison closed her eyes. She had never felt so completely alone before in her life. Big tears seeped out from under her closed lids and splashed on her lap.

Calvin couldn't find his clothes. There were tangles of twisted garments looking like rag bundles heaped all over the floor.

Giving up the attempt to find his own clothes, he hunted for anything to wear.

In the end, he came out ahead. He managed to find a nice pair of black woolen slacks and a hand-stitched suede smoking jacket.

Not a bad fit either. If nothing else, he had at least gotten himself some new clothes out of the party.

The problem of the overcoat was something else. All the coats that couldn't be squeezed into the hall closet were heaped on top of a radiator.

There was no use even bothering to look for his own coat. He'd never find it in that mess.

Instead, he just tried on all the men's overcoats in turn until he found one that was his size. It was a soft belted cashmere. Very snazzy. Very pawnable.

He was almost at the door when he saw her. She was sitting all alone and crying with her mouth open the way a child does.

Allison, yeah, Allison, that's what her name was. He went over to her.

"Allison?"

No answer.

"Allison, it's me, Calvin Staton."

Still no response.

He sat down on the arm of the chair and put his arm around her shaking shoulders. "It's a tough world, baby. Come on, I'll drive you home and you can tell me about it."

He took her hands in his and pulled her to her feet.

She wavered unsteadily for a moment then found her footing. "Lydia's mad at me," she told him solemnly.

"Who's Lydia. Oh, I think I know. I saw you with her earlier. You wanted to play house and she wouldn't let you. Well, anyway, let's get out of here and you can tell me all about it while I take you home."

Allison smiled beamingly up at him in gratitude. She took his hand and headed for the door.

"Hey," he called to her, "you better put some clothes on first."

CHAPTER SEVEN

The cold night air cleared her head a little. She paused for a moment to orient herself.

Where was she and who was this man?

She remembered. Lydia had left the party. Lydia hadn't wanted her to come along. She said she wouldn't be coming home until tomorrow and she didn't care what happened to Allison in the meanwhile.

Desolate numbness settled like a lead weight on Allison's heart.

Calvin's car was a beat-up old Hudson. There were dents and scratches all over it. One of the rear doors was tied on with rope. Rust was eating a lacework pattern like a hem around the edge of the body.

He slid in from the passenger's side first.

"Door on the other side doesn't work," he explained.

She noticed that he had left the keys in the ignition. Why not? No one would want to steal a wreck like this.

They drove through Central Park. It had snowed earlier in the evening. Now the park was wrapped in a blanket of purity.

It was incredibly quiet. Only the tops of the tall buildings along Central Park West, visible above the trees, reminded one that this was New York City.

"It's perfectly beautiful," Allison said.

"Nothing is perfect," Cal replied bitterly.

She let that one go.

They were in the Village within a very few minutes. Calvin drove down Greenwich Avenue without slackening his speed.

"Hey, this is where I live," she reminded him.

"I know. I thought we'd go up to my place for some coffee first. I only live a couple of blocks away."

"Well..."

"Skip the demure bit," he interrupted her. "I'm just inviting you up to my apartment for some coffee. Anything else is up to you."

Lydia was with a man. Lydia didn't care what she did.

"O.K.," she agreed.

Calvin's apartment on Cornelia Street proved to be a single room, not overly large, with an alcove kitchen. The whole place was painted black, even the ceiling.

A mattress and box spring lay on the floor. The sheets were yellow with age and grime. The bed looked as if it hadn't been made in weeks.

There was no closet. Shirts and jackets were hanging from nails driven into the back of the door. Underwear and socks were strewn about the room on the floor, chairs, bed, dresser, everywhere.

A single window looked out on the street. A rickety secretary was set up in front of it. There was an uncovered typewriter on the make-shift desk.

"I don't see any easels. Do you work in a studio?" she asked.

"Huh?"

"I thought you said you were an artist."

"Oh, I probably did. I'm not," he said.

"You talk and look like one."

"That's because I'm really a writer. Unsuccessful painters and unsuccessful writers all look alike."

"What do you write?"

"Did. I haven't written anything in over a year."

"Why?"

"They call it writer's block. Can't get the words out of my head and down on paper. When I could, I wrote novels. Mostly cheap things for the trash paperback market."

"Have you tried to get over your block?"

"All the time." He shifted his feet uncomfortably. "I better see about making us some coffee."

While he was busy in the kitchen, Allison went over to his desk.

There was a sheet of paper in the typewriter. She bent closer to look at it. It was blank except for one word typed in capital letters, dead center in the middle of the page.

CRAP

Cal came in with two chipped mugs of steaming coffee. He set them down on the floor in front of the bed and waited for her to join him.

Allison hesitated for a brief moment. There really was nowhere else to sit except on the bed. Everything else was piled high with clothing and books.

As soon as they were seated, he asked, "I didn't see you with any guys tonight. Don't you make it with men?"

"That's rather a personal question for you to ask, don't you think? After all, we hardly know each other."

"Oh, come off it," he said disgustedly. "If you're going to give me a hard time you might as well leave right now."

Go out there? Into the cold night? Alone?

"I've been to bed with a man."

"Well, three cheers for you. What do you have to act like it's such a big deal for?"

Allison took a sip of coffee instead of replying.

Calvin drained the last from his coffee cup. He wiped his mouth against his forearm and leaned back against the wall, his hands folded behind his head.

"What's with the les bit?" he asked abruptly.

Shocked embarrassment hit Allison like a kick in the back of her skull. "What do you mean?" she asked in a little voice.

"You live with that dyke with the blonde hair?"

"Yes."

"No kidding." He seemed to consider this deeply for a few minutes. "She digs guys. You too?"

"Sometimes."

"But you prefer it with girls?"

"I don't know," she answered truthfully.

"Come here." Cal put his hand on her shoulder and drew her back on the bed. She lay against his chest, listening to his heart beat. "Tell me about it."

Incredibly, Allison found herself pouring out the whole story to Cal. He was silent. She told him everything, the glory of being loved by Lydia and the pain and humiliation. Somehow she knew Cal wouldn't be shocked by her story.

When she was finished he had only one thing to say. "Jesus," Cal breathed.

He couldn't have said anything more appropriate. All sympathy and understanding was summarized in that one word. Allison felt closer to him in that moment than she had ever felt toward any man.

"Cal, will you do me a favor?"

"Depends. What?"

"Would you ... that is, if you don't mind ... after what I've just told you ... would you ... kiss me?" she finished breathlessly.

"Don't be an ass, Allison. Of course I'll kiss you. But first I want to set a few things straight. I don't know what kind of people you're accustomed to but I want to let you know that I'm me, Calvin Robert Staton. And I go for you even if you've got yourself all mixed up with a dyke. Frankly, I don't give two damns what you do when you're away. It's what happens when we're together that counts."

"You like me, Cal?"

"You bet I do, baby."

As his face came close to hers, his beard tickled and scratched her face at the same time. She felt almost as if she were going to sneeze.

When their lips met she forgot about the beard. Cal's tongue snaked out between his teeth. He licked at the tender lining of her mouth.

She caressed his tongue with her own. Over, around, under and over again. It was magnificent. Only their mouths existed in a vast void. Their tongues caressed each other in a flickering dance of passion.

He moved his hand.

"No! Not that."

"Why not, for Christ's sake?"

"I don't know. Just please don't."

"Relax, baby," Cal said cynically. "I'm not about to rape you. You won't get anything from me you don't want."

Allison stared at her hands lying folded in her lap. "I'm sorry."

"The hell you are. I've got news for you, baby. You're not just queer, you're a C.T. also."

"What's a C.T.?"

He told her.

"No, Cal. I wouldn't do that to you. I like you ... a lot. It's just that ... I don't know what it is. I'm all mixed up."

"Sure, baby, forget about it. For now. Want some more coffee?"

She glanced at her watch. Five in the morning. Lydia wouldn't be home yet.

"Love some."

While Cal was in the kitchen, Allison lay back on the bed and thought about what had happened.

She hadn't been lying. She did like him. He was rude and uncomplimentary and arrogant. But still she found him terribly attractive.

Then why not let him make love to her? Hell, Lydia wouldn't care. She always said she would never be jealous of a man. And God knows, Lydia had herself arranged it so that Allison had sex with a lot of the men.

She hadn't wanted any of them to touch her. And here she was with a guy who really got her worked up and she was pulling a virgin bit. It didn't make sense.

It did, though, in a screwy kind of a way. Lydia pushed her toward men because she knew Allison didn't like them. She might not feel the same way if Allison started getting something out of it.

There was more than a little truth in that. It was funny when you thought about it; Lydia was perfectly willing for her to go to bed with someone else so long as she didn't enjoy herself.

Lydia was afraid. The thought struck Allison like a sudden burst of light. It was incredible to think of it. Lydia, always so poised and self-assured, was afraid that Allison might leave her if she found someone else who satisfied her in bed.

Now it all made sense. Of course she couldn't go all the way with Cal. That would be like betraying Lydia.

Lydia was out having a ball with Bill. She didn't know if Allison was alive or dead and she cared less.

"I've come to a conclusion," Cal said as he came in with the coffee. "I've decided you really do go for me."

Of all the presumptuous self-conceit! It was true though. From the moment they met she had felt an hypnotic attraction. He was intelligent and understanding and decadent and evil. Cal Staton had the sinister attraction of a snake.

"And I also decided," he continued, "that you're a real female type female. The kind they don't hardly make any more. You're an anachronism. A submissive woman who needs a dominating man to tell her what to do." He lit a cigarette and flipped the match vaguely in the direction of the window.

"You Tarzan, me Jane," Allison sneered.

"You slave girl, me maharajah," he corrected. "You like to be pushed around, I'm willing to oblige."

"Big of you."

"Yes, I think it is."

"Suppose I don't want to?"

"You will," he spoke with complete surety. "Just as soon as you catch on that you've got no choice in that matter."

"May I at least drink my coffee before we start playing games?"

"Sure, I believe in being a benevolent despot."

He handed her a mug of coffee and picked up the other for himself. Allison noticed that her cup was smeared with lipstick around the brim. He hadn't washed the mug before putting fresh coffee into it.

They drank in silence. Allison didn't really want any coffee. She just sipped at it for something to do.

Cal drained his cup. "Here," he said, handing her his mug, "take these out to the kitchen and wash them."

"Do you mind if I at least finish my own first?"

"Yes, as a matter of fact, I do. You've had enough time. If you haven't finished it that's your tough luck. Now, get going."

She went.

When she came back from the kitchen she found him stretched out on the bed. His clothes were off.

The mattress on which he lay was bare. He had rolled all the sheets and blankets in a heap off the foot of the bed.

Cal didn't look at her. He just lay at perfect ease, watching the swirling patterns of blue smoke rising from his cigarette.

Allison was appalled by his thinness. There wasn't a drop of fat on him. The hard knots of his muscles bulged up, creating sinewy lumps in his olive skin. She could see the rise and fall of each separate rib as he breathed.

In spite of his thinness, he was good-looking. The combination of light blue eyes and blonde hair and beard was striking against his dark skin. He looked strong too.

He twisted his head to the side and grinned at her. "I'm waiting for you to take your clothes off. I don't like to be kept waiting, Allison."

A terrible excitement coursed through her. It was crazy, insane.

"I don't want to."

"Did I ask you?" Cal turned away from her and went back to studying smoke patterns.

"It's not that. Not really that," she admitted.

"What is it then?"

"I'm frightened. Suppose I get pregnant?"

"Best thing that could happen to you. Having a baby would make you stop thinking about yourself all the time."

She thought about it. She wanted him as much as he wanted her. More probably. And it would be hell just going home unsatisfied.

She was curious too. This was the first time she had ever really wanted a man to make love to her. She was sure nothing would happen. She'd be left unsatisfied as usual. But, still, maybe. Maybe this would be the time.

Other women experienced ecstasy in a man's arms. Why shouldn't she? It was wrong, unfair.

As if he sensed the struggle going on in her mind, Cal said, "Peel. Now, This instant."

She lowered herself to the bed. She was sitting next to his legs. One hand moved upward slowly. It came to rest on the top button of her blouse. She toyed with the button. Then undid it.

Cal was watching her. She was aware of it and she was pleased that her body was full and lush and young.

She unhooked her bra. Her breasts burst forth from their prison like eager ripe melons. When she had her slacks and panties off, she was proud of her flat stomach and the rounded slope of her hips.

She knelt on the edge of the bed, naked. Cal hadn't moved.

"Cal, suppose I do get pregnant? Have you ever thought about getting married?"

"I was married once. My wife died. That was a long time ago. Once was enough for me. I'll never marry again."

"Didn't you meet any women ever besides your wife you thought of marrying?"

"No. Besides, I don't think any woman would like to hook herself up with a guy like me."

"Why not? I should think a lot of women would want to marry you."

"For my money, baby?" Cal smiled scornfully to himself. "I'll show you what women want from me."

"I'm so mixed up," she moaned.

"You think too much," he said as he sat up on the bed. He pulled her down beside him. "Just feel, baby. Just let yourself feel."

Passion flooded through her. She wanted it so badly.

This time, this one time let it happen, she prayed. Let me feel what other women do. Please, God, just this once. I don't want anything more than other women have. They can love a man. I want to, too. I can't go through the rest of my life living in a shadowed world. I want to be normal, to feel what other women feel with a man. Lord, please let it happen.

She hadn't realized that she had been talking out loud. Cal lifted his head from her breast.

"You'll make it," he promised her. "This time you'll make it. I'll show you how."

She didn't know what to do. He had to show her.

She moved slowly, wincing as the pain grew. Then she tensed and stopped. No, she couldn't go through with it.

Suddenly, Allison whimpered in delight.

She burst apart. Rockets of ectasy careened crazily. The cosmos split apart.

It was nearly noon when she left him. A dull day, the sun covered by heavy rolling clouds. A grey light spread over the city, making it seem later than it actually was. The dirty heaps of snow on the curbs added to the gloom.

Allison hurried down the street. It wasn't likely that Lydia would be home yet. After a night like last night, she probably would spend most of the day sleeping it off at Valerie's. Still, if Lydia did get home first, if she were there now and wondering where Allison was, the consequences could be highly unpleasant.

Cal had been sleeping when she left him. He hadn't even awakened when she slipped out of the bed and put her clothes on. Even when she bent down to kiss him before leaving, he had gone right on sleeping.

That had hurt. The least he could have done would have been to stay awake long enough to say goodbye. Of course, he couldn't really be blamed. The night couldn't have meant as much to him as it did to her.

How was he to know? A man couldn't be expected to understand how a woman would feel. It was probably nothing more than a good roll in the hay for him. For Allison—well, for her it was something different—something very much more.

No man had ever done that to her before. She had tried. Again and again, with all kinds of men. Some had been gentle and adept, others rough and demanding. None had made her realize the wondrous delights her body could provide.

Then Cal had made love to her. And everything had been different. It was as if her body was not the same one the other men had touched. Cal had made something new of it. He had brought it to life, given birth to it in a way.

Afterward, when the dizziness subsided and the world came back into focus, Allison had hardly been able to realize that it had finally happened. Calvin Staton, a man she barely knew, a rude, arrogant man, had given her ecstasy.

Only Lydia had been able to do that before. And even that hadn't been quite the same. Always she had been left with a feeling that some part of her hadn't been reached, some deep need hadn't been satisfied.

Calvin had satisfied her completely.

Not just once but many times. All through the night and early morning they had made love. And each time it had been the same. Allison climbed to the peaks of desire to then descend in long shuddering waves of delight.

It was funny, after all those years of feeling nothing here she was suddenly responding normally time after time. Cal had a simple explanation for it. "The cork's out now," he said.

It was natural that he should fall asleep. The long hours of love-making had exhausted him. Even Allison was tired. Wonderful as it had been, her body demanded rest from all the exertion.

She hadn't slept. Her mind was too filled with the wonder of what had happened for sleep to come. Instead, she had lain on the bed with her eyes closed and her body relaxed and thought about Calvin.

He slept soundly beside her. His arm around her shoulders.

She took a peculiar delight in just listening to the quiet rhythm of his breathing. She could feel the pulse beating in his arm behind her neck. It seemed miraculous that he slept and breathed like every human being. Somehow, because he had accomplished what no one else had been able to do, she half expected him to be different from other mortals, more god-like somehow.

The smell of him was lovely to her, the slightly sour odor of a man. His right hand was resting on her shoulder. The faint perfume of her own body clung to it.

This reminder of his caress filled her with feelings of loving gratitude. She turned her head to kiss his hand. Her eyes fell on the watch strapped to his wrist.

It was eleven o'clock.

Good Lord, what if Lydia had already come home! She'd catch holy hell for not being there. And poor Prufrock. The dog had been alone in the apartment for over twenty hours. He hadn't been taken out for a walk since lunch time the day before. The poor beast's bladder was probably nearly bursting.

She sprang out of bed and into her clothes. No time for a shower or even a quick washup. Anyway, she didn't know where the bathroom was.

Calvin was still sleeping soundly. She sat down on the bed next to him for a moment. He slept nicely, not snoring or with his mouth open like a lot of men. He looked peaceful and happy.

She reached down to the foot of the bed and pulled a blanket free from the heap on the floor. She covered him with it. As she tucked the edges in, she noticed again how frightfully thin he was. Poor guy probably hadn't had a decent meal in God knows how long. Living alone in this miserable room he probably made do with coffee and canned goods most of the time.

Allison smiled to herself. It amused her to find herself thinking about the meals she would cook for Calvin. How he would ridicule her if he knew she felt maternal towards him.

She bent down to kiss him goodbye. Their mouths met. Cal sighed softly, still sleeping. Allison brushed her mouth against his again. His lips tasted so good.

She felt the familiar warmth stealing through her. A pulse began to beat low in her body.

She jumped to her feet. No time for that now. Besides, she was acting like a pig. Three times in one night ought to be enough for anyone.

As she was walking down the stairs she remembered that they hadn't discussed when they would meet again. There had been more immediate things occupying them. Oh well, Cal knew where she lived. Even if he didn't have the telephone number, he had only to walk the few blocks to her apartment to contact her. Maybe he'd even come over that evening after he woke up. It never occurred to her that he might not want to be with her again as much as she looked forward to seeing him.

As she climbed the stairs she could hear Prufrock whimpering and snuffling. He recognized her step and was knocking himself out with eagerness.

She unlocked the door. Prufrock, usually so calm and dignified, jumped up on her, almost knocking her over. He laved her face with wet kisses. Then he followed her into the foyer, running around her in circles, mad with joy.

The excitement was too much for him. Self-control gave way to joy. There was a thin yellowish river on the hardwood floor.

Prufrock let his stump of a tail droop. He lay down on the floor, his whole body shivering and cringing. If it's possible for a dog to look that way, Prufrock's face wore an expression of fear and humiliation.

Allison bent down to pat him. "That's all right, boy. You didn't do it deliberately. It was an accident. I'm not going to punish you."

One thing was certain, Lydia hadn't come home yet. The dog would never have had an accident if he had been taken out.

Allison hung her coat in the closet. "I'll take you out just as soon as I've bathed and changed my clothes," she promised the dog. A few minutes more wouldn't hurt him. And she just had to get out of those grimy clothes.

CHAPTER EIGHT

The Doberman was all aired and fed. The apartment was in order and Allison had bathed and put on fresh clothes. It was still only one o'clock in the afternoon. Lydia still hadn't shown up yet but that didn't mean much. She might not be coming home until nearly dinner time. The long afternoon stretched out before Allison with nothing to do.

She didn't feel in the least bit tired. Odd, after not sleeping and all that sex. Yet she felt good, alive and tingly and full of energy.

But it's all probably a temporary illusion, she told herself. Better to try and take a nap while I can. Lydia might feel like going out tonight and she'll be furious if I'm too tired.

She forced herself to lie still on the big bed. It was obvious to her that sleep would never come, she was too filled with energy. But, minutes after she closed her eyes, she fell into a deep sleep.

It was dark when she awoke. She switched on the lamp beside the bed. The small bulb cast a soft light over the room, making it look warm and cosy. Allison stretched luxuriously.

She could hear rain beating against the windowpanes. Gusts of wind howled. It was a good night to stay home. A good night to just laze around and listen to music.

She was too comfortable to get up and put records on the phonograph. Instead, she turned on the bedside radio.

A medley of schmaltzy show tunes was being played by one of those big orchestras with lots of violins. Real cornball stuff and just right for her mood.

The record came to an end. An announcer cut in to announce the station's call letters and, "Now, time for our eight o'clock news summary."

Eight o'clock! She had no idea she had been sleeping that long. And where the hell was Lydia? It wasn't like her to stay away *this* long without calling.

Allison was worried. Lydia was more capable of taking care of herself than any three other people on earth put together. There was really no need to be concerned. But still, something might have happened to her. What with the liquor and the marijuana, Lydia had been pretty high last night. She might have had an accident with the car.

Better to check with Valerie first. Could be that Lydia was still sleeping it off.

She dialled the number. The phone rang three times. Then a voice cut in to inform her that the number she had dialled had been temporarily disconnected and that this was a recorded announcement.

Allison hung up the phone. She wondered why Valerie had had the phone taken out. Couldn't be that she hadn't paid her bill. Valerie made a small fortune for herself from her combination brothel and hotel.

Lydia had been a client of Valerie's for years. She really dug the crazy setup up there. She liked feeling that she was really one of the whores Valerie kept available in the rooms which men rented for an hour or more.

Allison thought of calling Bill. He might know what had happened to Lydia. He wouldn't be home at this hour. He was due on stage in a few minutes. There was just a chance she could catch him before the curtain went up.

She called backstage at the theatre where he was appearing. No luck. Bill Roman was not at the theatre, his understudy would be taking his place for the night.

She was really in a panic now. Bill wouldn't miss a performance unless something really drastic had happened. And most likely Bill was detained for the same reason as Lydia.

They must have been in an accident. Lydia might be lying in a hospital right this moment injured or possibly dying.

Allison started calling hospitals, asking if Lydia were registered there. She had no idea of which hospital would be the correct one. The only thing to do was go down the list in the telephone book, calling each one.

It was a formidable list, calling them all took her well over an hour. There were over one hundred public and private hospitals in New York City alone. For all she knew, Bill and Lydia might have taken a ride out of town and gotten into an accident on the road. They might be anywhere.

As she called hospital after hospital and was told that Lydia Stone was not a patient, Allison's sense of guilt grew. She should have been home last night after the party. She should have been available if Lydia had needed her.

Maybe Lydia had telephoned while she was with Cal. Possibly this wouldn't have happened to Lydia if Allison had been able to talk to her. Maybe Lydia had gotten hurt racing home because she was worried about Allison.

The hospital idea was a dud. She called the last one on the list. Lydia wasn't a patient there.

Allison hung up the phone. She didn't know what to do next. Lydia needed her and she hadn't been available.

It was all her fault. She didn't love Lydia enough and that's why this happened. God was punishing her. She deserved it. After all Lydia had done for her, she had turned her back on her.

She had been with Calvin, letting him make love to her, to her body that rightfully belonged only to Lydia.

Worst of all, she remembered the terrible thoughts she had had about Lydia last night. It was horrible of her to think such things. She saw evil in other people because of her own badness.

Yes, there was no doubt about it, she was evil. She had always been. Even as a little girl she was always doing bad things. Mother punished her because she was bad. It was only right.

Then she had been bad to Lydia and Lydia had had to punish her. Only the punishment wasn't enough, she went on being bad because there was something so depraved about her nothing could change her. First her mother had loved her and then Lydia. And because they loved her, she had hurt them with her sinfulness.

Good girls didn't go to bed with a man unless they were married to him. Everyone knew that. And she had gone to bed with Calvin Staton. And because she was so bad, she had enjoyed it. She had reveled in sinning so much that she hadn't even cared about what was happening to Lydia. Lydia who loved her.

Allison hardly knew when the headache began. Her whole being was wracked with guilty pain. The pain in her skull was only a little worse than the rest.

The headache grew with terrific speed. With it came nausea and dizziness. She groped her way to the bathroom.

Her guts were spilling out. She knelt before the toilet bowl spewing out the badness inside her. If only she could keep it up until it was all out and she was clean inside.

There was nothing more to come up. Still the contractions tore at her tortured guts. The pain was too much. She would never be able to complete her purification.

Her head was throbbing. The spasms of pain came like the rhythmic beating of a drummer knocking against her skull.

Then there was blackness.

Consciousness came back slowly. She felt the chill of a damp cloth on her forehead. The sharp smell of vinegar made her nostrils contract.

Too soon to open her eyes. A few minutes more rest before facing the world again.

She could hear someone breathing in the room and sense his presence beside her.

"Allison? Allison, are you all right?"

She opened her eyes.

Paul Spencer was sitting beside her on the bed. His worried frown gave way to an expression of relief as he saw her open her eyes.

"What happened?" she asked.

"I knocked on the door. When you didn't answer I got worried. I knew you were home because I tried to call you and the phone was busy.

"I put my ear to the door. I thought I heard someone being sick. So I put my shoulder to the door. After a few shoves, the lock gave.

"I found you in the bathroom. You were lying on the floor, unconscious. I picked you up and carried you in here to the bed. There were no smelling salts in the medicine cabinet so I soaked a cloth with vinegar and put it on your head. It did the trick.

"Are you all right now?" he concluded. "Should I call a doctor?"

"No, I don't need a doctor. I'll be o.k."

She sat up. Why had she gotten sick? It had been so long since she had had a migraine attack. What had brought this one on?

"Lydia!" Allison screamed.

"That's what I came to see you about," Paul said.

"Where is she? Take me to her." She started rising from the bed.

Paul grabbed her by the shoulders and pushed her back down. "Calm yourself," he said. "You'll do no one any good by getting hysterical. Lydia is all right. She's not sick or anything like that, if that's what you're thinking."

"Then why isn't she home?"

Paul sighed deeply before continuing. "She can't come home. Not yet. I'm working on getting her back in a few days."

"For Christ's sake, will you tell me what happened?" Allison wailed in exasperation.

"Lydia's in trouble. She and Bill Roman were at Valerie's last night when the place was raided. They hauled Lydia in with the other girls. It was a first offense and I might have been able to fix things up for her right away but she was high on marijuana and she got out of hand. She resisted arrest and generally made herself obnoxious. The police aren't in any mood to do her any favors as a result.

"She used the one phone call she was allowed to call me—because I'm her lawyer," he added. "She asked me to call you. I tried all night but there was no answer. Anyway, I'm pulling as many strings as I can to get Lydia out. Until I can, she's in the Women's House of Detention.

"I saw her this morning. She said for me to tell you that you should come see her posing as her sister. She was very worried because you weren't home. I didn't have a chance to call all afternoon because I was working on her case. I came here the moment I had a spare minute."

It was agonizing. The Women's House of Detention was only two blocks away on the corner of Greenwich Avenue and Sixth Avenue. Lydia was so near. And Allison couldn't be with her. Not until visitor's day.

"Do you have enough money?" Paul asked.

"I'll get along."

"Dammit, Allison, don't start pulling a proud martyr bit with me. Tell me straight, how much cash do you have on hand?"

"I don't know."

"Well, look in your wallet and find out." Paul sounded as if he was at the end of his patience.

She searched through her purse, her pockets and the bureau drawer where Lydia often threw small change. Added all together, she had ten dollars and thirty-five cents.

"No telling when Lydia will be able to give you some more. Here," Paul took out his wallet, "this is all I can spare for now. I'll get more for you in a few days if it's necessary."

Paul left. It was after midnight and he had to drive all the way out to Montauk.

Allison put the forty dollars Paul had given her into her wallet. She didn't like taking his money. He was in no position to throw money away with a wife and kids to support.

Paul was coming through for Lydia as usual. Poor sap, he knocked himself out for Lydia and all she did was treat him like a slave.

Loving her so much it must have killed him to have her marry his own brother. And after the divorce, when Lydia started running wild, having affairs with one man after another, Paul knew all about it. Lydia delighted in torturing him with endless recitations about her sexual life. Paul never wavered in his love for her.

Paul knew that Allison was Lydia's lover. He was willing to give up his marriage, his career, his whole way of life for her. But Lydia chose a woman to live with.

Allison knew that Paul hated her. It was perfectly justified. There was nothing personal in his hatred. It was the natural outgrowth of his jealousy and envy.

Despite his loathing, Paul was kind to Allison. He even gave her money he could use for himself. All for love of Lydia. Because Lydia wanted him to be nice to Allison.

That deep a capacity for love was a rare thing. Paul embodied all the qualities of steadfastness and gallantry that most men lacked. He was more like a romantic hero out of a book than an ordinary human being.

Yet, Allison couldn't suppress a feeling of contempt toward him.

Allison embarked on her new regime the next day. Like most repentant sinners, she overdid the penance bit. The idea was to change herself over completely. From the ungrateful sinner who had been responsible for Lydia's arrest to a virtuous paragon of righteousness.

There was no logic behind it. No matter how you looked at it, you couldn't hold Allison responsible. Lydia got herself in trouble because she insisted on staying in Valerie's brothel.

Lydia had been going there with her various lovers long before she had even met Allison. She knew the risk she was taking. Fool's luck had kept her from getting caught in a raid until now.

Yet, why had Lydia been arrested on this particular night? Allison knew the answer to that one. She knew it with a deep conviction that was close to faith even though it didn't make any sense logically.

Lydia was arrested that night because of Allison's badness. She was responsible. It was up to Allison to reform so Lydia could get out of prison. She would never sin again so that Lydia wouldn't be hurt.

Allison drew up a list of resolutions and carried them out with fanatic intensity. The apartment was cleaned until it was almost sterile. She waxed the floors and furniture and polished them until they gleamed.

Allison examined every piece of clothing Lydia wore. She made sure all the buttons were tightly sewn on. Places where stitching was just beginning to give, she ripped the thread out of and re-sewed.

She washed all their laundry by hand and ironed it. The Chinese laundryman across the street did a much better job but

Allison wanted to do the work herself. She took pleasure in sav-ing Lydia's money for her.

Prufrock was Lydia's dog so he came in for the same kind of treatment. Allison tried to be good to him as best she knew how. In consequence, the Doberman was walked until the pads on his feet were sore. Allison indulged him at mealtime wildly. She fed him pastries and sweets as treats. The rich food upset his stomach and one night Prufrock was so sick Allison had to call the veterinarian.

Her attitude toward herself was the exact opposite. Discipline and self-denial were her mottoes. She bought a big bag of fruits and vegetables for her meals. That was all she ate. And she was careful to keep the portions small enough to leave her still a little bit hungry all the time.

She put away all the brightly colored clothes she owned and only wore those of somber hue. Her favorite outfit now was a black turtlenecked sweater worn with black leotards and grey desert boots. Her long black hair was brushed flat along the sides and pulled back into a ponytail. The only reason she didn't have her hair cut off was that Lydia liked it long.

Makeup was completely out. After a few days of going about in the near freezing weather that way, her lips became so chapped they bled. After that she allowed a light application of pale pink lipstick for necessity's sake.

Cal was, naturally, item number one on the list of the forbid-den. Allison accused herself of sinning if she so much as thought about him. As far as she was concerned, Calvin Staton was dead.

He came to see her one afternoon. When the downstairs bell rang, Allison pressed the answering buzzer, thinking it might be the mailman delivering a package.

The knocking on the door to the apartment came surpris-ingly soon afterward, considering the four flights of stairs.

"Who is it?" Allison asked before unlocking the door.

"Allison?"

"Yes."

"This is Cal, Cal Staton. Open up. I want to talk to you."

Allison leaned against the doorjamb, her heart beating wildly. "Go away. I don't want to talk to you."

"Come on, will ya, I only want to see you for a minute. Open up the door and talk to me. Then I'll go away."

"No," she hissed. "Go away. And don't try to see me again. I never want to see you again."

"For Christ's sake!" Cal muttered a string of curses. "At least tell me what this is all about? What did I do? Why won't you at least talk to me?"

There was no answer.

Cal put his ear to the door. He could hear breathing on the other side.

"Allison, I know you're there. Believe me, I don't want to bother you. I won't force myself on you if you don't want me. I wouldn't do anything to harm you for all the world, you believe that, don't you? Allison, Allison, are you in some sort of trouble?"

"No, I'm not in trouble. I—I can't explain. Not now. Please, Cal, go away and let me alone. It's better this way—for both of us."

He waited in silence.

From the other side of the locked door he heard the sound of a body slumping to the floor. Then he heard her crying. Between sobs, she whispered his name. "Cal, Cal, oh ..."

He pounded on the door with his fists. "Allison, I'm not going away from here until you tell me why you won't see me!"

"Never!" she shouted tearfully.

After a long while, when the sound of crying had stopped and still he could get no answer to his questions, Cal left.

That night, when Allison visited Lydia, she poured the whole story out to her. The half hour allowed at the Women's House of Detention was hardly long enough. Allison related everything that had transpired between Cal Staton and herself as fast as she could. When she finished, she slumped back in her chair, exhausted by her *mea culpa*.

She waited, her eyes half-closed with exhaustion, for Lydia's condemnation. To her immense suprise, Lydia laughed.

"Oh, you naive child, you poor sweet baby," Lydia said between gasps of laughter. "Did you really think I'd be angry? Oh, baby, baby," she went off into fresh peals of laughter. When she had recovered herself she said, "Look, I've always told you I didn't mind if you made it with guys, didn't I?"

"Yes," Allison agreed.

"And I've never liked it that you didn't go for men. It made me feel creepy. I mean, as if there were something abnormal about you. So now you had a ball with a man. I'm glad. Really I am."

"I should have known you would be," Allison said bitterly.

"Now don't get nasty, honey." Lydia raised one eyebrow provocatively. "I'm not about to throw you to the wolves. You're still my baby and no one else's. The point is that I don't give a tinker's damn about this Calvin slob just because you went to bed with him and enjoyed it. What matters is that you stay true to me in your heart. I don't want to share your love with anyone. Be honest with me, Allison. Do you care for him?"

"No! Oh, Lydia, no! You're the only one I love! The only one I'll ever love!"

"Make sure you stay that way," Lydia said in a voice that was heavy with menace.

The visiting period was over.

Allison couldn't shake off the feeling that all was not as it seemed. Lydia's laugh had been too hearty, almost forced. Was she really as unconcerned as she acted?

It didn't seem right. This hadn't been a case of simple sexual release. Cal had touched something deep in her.

And Lydia was far too perceptive a woman not to have sensed that. Why was she playing it so cool?

CHAPTER NINE

CALVIN STATON

Calvin Staton, twenty-nine years old, five feet eleven inches tall, weighing one hundred forty one pounds, placed the bristled end of his shaving brush against the mirror and drew an S in lather on the glass. One letter was all he had room for. The rest of the word could be filled in by anyone who would wonder why a man would soap over his own reflected image.

He turned on the faucet in the sink and dunked his head under it, letting the chill water wash away the lather on his face.

To hell with it! If anybody didn't like his beard they could go take a flying leap for themselves. He'd be damned if he'd go through this routine every day.

He started to clean off his shaving utensils and then decided the hell with them too. He threw them into the wastebasket.

Shaving is a question of current fashion, he reflected. There was a time when a clean shaven man was looked upon as eccentric. Why should I be a slave to transient tastes in fashion? To keep the razor blade manufacturers in business? They can go to hell too.

He picked up a rag which was draped over the side of the bathtub and washed the lather off the mirror with it.

Now he could see himself. Not exactly a pleasing sight. He was too thin. Cal ran the flat of his palms down either side of his bare chest. The ribs stuck out like something in a natural history museum.

And his beard did look crummy. Not bad enough to shave off. Just scraggly and moth-eaten.

He searched around the bathroom for something to fix it up with. There was a pair of manicure scissors on the floor behind the toilet. He picked them up and examined them. They were rusty around the hinges from lying on the damp floor. He scraped the rust off with his thumbnail.

He dried the mirror off with a towel. Now he could see himself again. He started the laborious job of trimming his beard with the tiny manicure scissors.

Cal shrugged himself into his overcoat. He paused for a moment before going out to admire himself in the mirror. Yeah, the fuzz looked good. He ran his hand lovingly over the neatly pointed beard.

He ran lightly down the stairs. The short walk to Greenwich Avenue took him less than five minutes.

Now the hard part began. Allison Fuller lived somewhere on this street. Cal remembered that much from the night when he had started out to drive her home from Bill Roman's party. Exactly where she lived he didn't know.

There was only one way to find out. Read the names on the mailboxes in each and every building until he found the right one.

He should have asked her for her phone number. God only knew what she thought of him now. A girl didn't like it when she went to bed with you and you didn't even ask to see her again.

Maybe she understood. Maybe she knew that he wanted to be with her again. And maybe she wouldn't mind that he hadn't come around right away.

It wasn't because he didn't want to be with her. Hell no. As soon as he woke up and saw that she was no longer lying beside him he had missed her.

The party that night and all the sex after it had knocked him out. It was already after midnight when he woke up. A couple of times before he had slept a full day after smoking pot. He had always felt great when he woke up.

He woke up that night full of energy. He flung open the bedroom window and let the cold air play on his naked body.

It was a nice night. Cold and bright. The stars shone clearly in the frozen sky. A great night for a long walk. Cal thought about picking up Allison and taking her for a stroll. The trucks would be loading down along West Street in a few hours and they could watch all the frantic activity and have themselves a fine time for free.

He knew Allison would enjoy the spectacle as much as he did. But would she enjoy his ringing her bell at this hour of the night? Not too likely. Especially since she didn't live alone. Better put it off until tomorrow.

Instead, Cal dressed himself warmly in heavy Army surplus clothes and went for a walk alone. Harry, an old friend of his who worked as a dispatcher for one of the big nation-wide trucking outfits, was on duty that night. Because he had to stand out on the open platform all night in the bitter cold, Harry kept a bottle of rye handy. Cal joined him on the platform and the two men knocked the bottle off between them.

Harry's working hours ended shortly after dawn. Cal went with him to a joint on Bethune Street which catered to the truckers and dock workers. They ate huge breakfasts of ham, eggs, waffles, toast, hot cereal, fruit juice, muffins and coffee.

They left the restaurant tired and sleepy. The heated restaurant and all the food they had stashed away drained the last drop of energy from them.

Harry headed north toward the Eighth Avenue subway stop. He'd sleep most of the way up to his home in the Bronx and work up enough strength to make it with his wife when he got home. She liked to be awakened that way, said it made her feel good all the rest of the day.

Cal walked in the opposite direction toward his apartment on Cornelia Street. The muscles at the back of his legs ached with tiredness. When a cab passed he was tempted to hail it but the single dollar bill in his pocket stopped him.

There was about a dollar more in change lying around his apartment, he knew. Lousy mess for a grown man to get himself into. He had been broke many times in his life before but never this bad. And he hadn't any idea of where any more money would be coming from when the two bucks ran out.

He could get a job, of course. There was always something he could pick up to do for a little while that would carry him through. It wouldn't be the first time he had run errands for the uptown pushers to pick up a couple of bucks.

Or he could get himself a legitimate job. One of those blue suit and conservative tie jobs like most of the other stiffs in this world had. Cal hated to do that though. He hated the thought of the long hours of senseless labor that left him stiff with boredom, of the bullying bosses who made you feel like punching them on their supercilious noses, of the inane conversations that passed for friendliness in office men's rooms.

Much as he needed the money, it was wrong for him to take a regular job for financial reasons. No job would pay him as much as he could make from his writing. And if he worked he wouldn't have the time and energy for writing. Once he had figured out that the least amount of money he had ever made for writing a book was fifteen dollars an hour. No job would pay him that much.

So why didn't he stay home and write instead of boozing it up all night on the docks?

Why not?

For the same damn reason he hadn't been able to write a line for over a year now.

Because there had been a girl. A girl who had come into his life after he had knocked around for so many years he no longer believed there were such women. The girl had been lovely and kind and warm. She had been too wonderful, like a fawn arrested in flight, a splendor that cannot last.

The girl had loved Cal. They had married and moved into an apartment and the girl went around the apartment cleaning up or sat reading quietly while Cal pounded the typewriter. They were so happy.

Cal's work went well. He wrote a novel that was published by one of the big publishing houses. It was a book he was proud of and for once in his career, he used his own name on it. The book was never a best seller. It got decent reviews and it sold well enough so they didn't have to worry about money and even had enough to buy a new car.

The girl had taken the new car and driven to New Hampshire to visit her parents. It was bitter cold up there. The country roads weren't made to drive on. They were so seldom used that a layer of soft snow covered the ice underneath. It was wet, slippery snow. The car skidded a few times. She had to push the accelerator to the floor to make it up hills.

Coming down an incline, the rear wheels locked. The skid came to an end when the hood of the car burrowed into a huge snow bank at the side of the road. She tried pulling the car out by putting it in reverse and gunning the motor. After a while she gave it up. It was no use. The car hadn't budged an inch and the engine was already flooded with gas.

The girl opened the car door. The wind was so strong it was like someone was pushing against her. She had to use all her strength to get the car door open.

Overhead, electric power lines hummed an unheard song in the fury of the storm. They were brittle with the intense cold and the weight of the snow. Some of them sagged dangerously, swaying their white crested lengths in the wind.

A wire sank a fraction of an inch lower. The weight of the snow was straining its delicate tension. Along with its customary hum, the wire made a sound like an old man groaning.

The weight of the snow and the intense cold were too much. The wire snapped through the air in a magnificent curving leap.

The girl who was like a fawn never knew that the falling wire had draped itself across her shoulders as she stood leaning against the car.

He had been trying to ease the awful ache for the past year. Nothing had helped much. Liquor was better than anything else. At least if he drank enough, there were moments when he could think of his wife without wishing his own life had ended with hers.

He had to pull himself together. It was either that or cirrhosis of the liver and being carried from a Bowery flophouse in a wooden box to a grave in Potter's Field.

His money had gone on booze and women who looked a little bit like his wife or had a New England accent like hers or used the same perfume or had a way of holding their heads which reminded him of her. He had to get back to work.

Cal tried. It was no use. He was in a slump. Writer's block—an occupational hazard like a hand injury for a pianist. He couldn't write. When he tried to, he ended up by either staring morosely at the blank sheet of paper in the typewriter or went out and got himself loaded.

Life was meaningless without his wife. Nothing seemed to matter.

Night followed day in a blur of reached for but never quite attained oblivion. Cal staggered around New York City, seeking forgetfulness in the myriad worlds apart which exist around the corner from each other in the city.

He lay in the arms of women willing and eager and with those whose services were for hire. There were fights in barrooms and dark alleyways. He could remember punching and getting slugged back in return. He couldn't remember what any of the arguments had been about nor the names and faces of the men he traded blows with.

There were the mornings when he woke up in tenement hallways with his head throbbing and his clothes a torn filthy mess. Standing up made the sidewalk rock from side to side like a ship in a rough sea. His tortured guts screamed for liquor. Cal staggered to the nearest saloon. He ordered neat shots of rye which he had difficulty lifting to his mouth because of the trembling in his hands.

The morning drink made him feel a little better. His body ceased writhing inside his skin like a prisoner jailed in a hairshirt straitjacket. And the rye cleared his mind too.

That wasn't good. He thought of his wife. Of happiness given and then snatched away by the capricious gods. Another drink...and another after that one. Pour the alcohol down his ravaged throat until his brain drowned in the stuff and memories of the girl he had married only floated on the surface like oil slick on a bottled-in-bond sea.

By this point he didn't even bother trying to write a line. His agent gave up on him and stopped trying to get him assignments. Cal borrowed money from everyone he knew. Every penny he could lay his hands on went for liquor.

He hadn't quite hit rock bottom yet, although he was well on his way. Luckily, just before starting the long binge, he had located a cheap room. For fifty bucks a month he had a place to flop in a neighborhood where they weren't too particular about what condition he came home in.

Some last small remnant of sense lurking around in the back of his brain had made him keep up his rent payments. The room on Cornelia Street wasn't much but it was his own. A man couldn't really be called a derelict as long as he had a place of his own to sleep in.

Cal only made it home a few times a week. Other times, the liquor caught up with him before he got there and he settled for any place where he could get out of the wind.

One night when he was fumbling with his key, trying to insert it in the keyhole which seemed to be creeping away as he reached for it, the door to his apartment swung open. Cal blinked in the sudden assault of light. The naked bulb which hung from a cord in the center of his room was turned on and the harsh light hurt his eyes.

"Come in, Cal. We've been waiting for you. The superintendent let us in," a man said.

Cal followed him into the room. He stared uncertainly at the man who had opened the door. He knew him from somewhere. The beefy face laced with a network of red lines was familiar to him. Even the man's deep, rumbling voice which seemed to come from the recesses of his bulging paunch, struck a cord of remembrance.

There was a woman sitting in the straight chair beside his desk. A thin, faded woman who would never see fifty again. Her gray streaked brown hair was caught up in a tight bun at the back of her head. Her lips were thin and tightly pressed together, the mouth of a woman who suffered patiently. She looked at Cal with eyes of a pale, washed-out blue. The rims were red from crying. Her nose was small and sharp, the nostrils edged with pink as though discolored from constant tears.

He knew both of them, the man and the woman. Cal tried hard to remember where and when in the life that had been his before the world had become compressed into a vast distillery he had met them.

His mother and father-in-law! Come all the way to New York from their New Hampshire farm to share with him the bittersweet memories which were all the three of them had left. Come to give and receive comfort with the man who, with them, had known the splendid pain of loving their daughter.

He sank to his knees with a wordless cry of pain and buried his head in his mother-in-law's lap.

The old woman ran trembling fingers of love through his matted, dirt-caked hair. "My boy," she crooned, "My poor baby boy."

The old people took a room in a nearby hotel. They couldn't afford it.

It didn't matter. Nothing was important enough to call them away until they had done what they could for their son-in-law. For weeks they thought of nothing else except helping Calvin Staton pull himself out of the hell they had found him in.

They nursed Cal through the drying-out period. When they saw that he was no longer a slave to alcohol and could face the world without its poisonous balm, they gave him what little money they had left and went back to New Hampshire.

The money was just a loan. Cal comforted himself with that thought even though he had no idea of when he'd be able to pay it back.

He was deeply humiliated. His wife's mother and father were good people. They lived sheltered lives among others who shared the same ideas. They had never before dealt with a human being turned rotten like a piece of fruit, shriveled and slimy with horrible incrustations.

He hated himself because he had appeared before them drunk and filthy. He would never let something like that happen again.

He still drank socially and sometimes enough to get a pleasant buzz on. There was no comparison with his previous dependency on the bottle.

January First was his deadline. At the beginning of the New Year Cal resolved that he was going to really buckle down, chain himself to the typewriter if need be and get some work done.

The New Year came and went. His writing still didn't flow and putting words on paper was like tearing a part of his guts out. For two solid weeks he kept himself seated in front of the typewriter. It was agony. Nothing came of it.

Bill Roman's party came along just at the right time. Cal needed a good excuse to goof off. I need a change of scene, he told himself. A little recreation will do me good.

And all the while that he was making excuses for himself, Cal knew that the party wouldn't change anything. He still wouldn't be able to write. No matter how many parties he went to, the thought of sitting down in front of the typewriter would still make him sick to his stomach.

But Bill Roman's party hadn't turned out quite the way he had expected it to. The girls and the pot and the booze were set out as if he had painted the scene in his imagination. Nothing there to help him write again.

Except for a girl he met at the party. A girl who was lost and confused as he had been. A girl named Allison Fuller who, for some reason he didn't quite understand, made him feel good and right about himself for the first time in ages.

There was a difference in him. Even just that one night with Allison had done a lot for him. He felt calmer, more sure of himself. Allison made him feel as if he was in control of his own destiny. It was quite a switch from letting the wind blow him from saloon to saloon.

The early morning breeze blew cold off the Hudson River. Cal hunched his shoulders against the wind. In spite of it, he felt warm inside.

Allison needs me, he thought. She's just about the craziest, most mixed-up broad I've ever met and she needs someone to help her. Someone who knows what they're doing, a guy who is already standing square on his own two feet who can help her stand on hers. It'll have to be someone who loves her too because that gal needs affection like a baby needs its bottle.

You're the guy for the job, Cal Staton, he told himself. Maybe he didn't love her yet but he sure had a mighty strong inclination in that direction. Time would make it more solid, he was sure.

And if he could help Allison, he could help himself. The conclusion was inescapable. Something had snapped in him since he met her. Some rottenness had gone out of his soul.

You can write again, Cal told himself. He didn't have to see the words on paper. Just knowing how he felt inside was enough. With the kind of attitude he had now he could make it.

Writing because of Allison and for Allison. He needed her as much as she needed him. Without her he was no good.

Cal quickened his steps. He was dog tired after the long night on the docks. But there was a fire burning inside him. This was no time for sleep. This was the time for action.

He searched among the clothes littering the room. Better not to look too much like a bum. At last he assembled an outfit that was respectable and reasonably clean.

Lou might not be in the office. Then he would have wasted precious hours going all the way up there. On the other hand, if he called first, Lou might be a little harder to convince. It was always easier for Cal to sell himself in person. He decided to risk it.

Subway fare cut his capital down to just under two dollars. If Lou couldn't get something for him right away he'd really be up the well known creek without a paddle.

He sat down on one of the red leather sofas while the receptionist announced him over the intercom.

"Cal Staton!" Lou's roar could be heard all over the office. "He dropped dead a year ago."

The receptionist was bewildered. She looked up at Cal for help.

He walked over to her desk and took the earphones from her.

"They forgot to bury me," he spoke softly into the phone.

"I'll be damned," Lou muttered. His voice rose to its customary roar again. "Why the hell didn't you call first?"

"I was afraid you wouldn't see me."

"Yeah, you were right about that. Cal, baby, I'll give it to you straight. I'm busy, up to my cheeks in work. I haven't got any time to sit around talking over old times. Are you drinking?"

"I'm not drunk if that's what you mean."

"You working on anything?"

"Not yet. That's what I came to see you about."

"Well, then why the hell don't you come in here instead of wasting my time with all this conversation?" Lou bawled.

Cal handed the headset back to the receptionist. Try as he would to appear nonchalant, he couldn't suppress the huge grin that spread across his face. Lou was still his agent and behind him all the way. He wouldn't have yelled like that if he wasn't on his side. Politeness toward a writer was his way of giving the brushoff.

It might have been only five minutes since he had last been in the office. Nothing had changed. Lou was still sitting behind a desk spilling over with manuscripts, contracts, letters, books, etc. It even seemed that the rolled up balls of paper spilling over the top of the wastebasket were the same ones.

If they could manufacture Lou pills, benzedrine would go off the market, Cal thought. As always, Lou emanated terrific energy and drive. He was hip-deep in ambition and no one resented it in him because he was so open about it. The essence of the whole man was contained in two bright blue eyes that penetrated right through every pretense and could see at a glance how your liver was holding up and what your sex life had been like in the past month.

"Enter the prodigal writer," Lou growled.

"There is more joy in heaven ..."

"Can it," Lou interrupted. "I've got the pitch already. What makes you think you're still able to write?"

Instead of answering, Cal let Lou come to his own conclusion.

"Stubborn son-of-a-bitch, aren't you?" Lou looked almost happy. "So what have you got in mind?"

"So what would you recommend?"

Lou swiveled around in his chair. He leaned his chin on his palm and sat staring out the window at the windows of the hotel across the street. Finally he spoke, his voice low and soft, still looking out the window. "Think you've got another book like the last one in you?"

"Dozens of them. I'm hot again, Lou. I'll give you a book now that'll make the last one look like chopped liver."

"So what are you standing around here for? Get out of here, you crummy bastard, and start writing!"

"I can't, Lou. Not right now."

"Why not?" Lou took a cigar out of the box on his desk and lit it. His expression was veiled, waiting.

"I'm broke, Lou. I need money. Right away."

"I don't give advances unless there's a check coming in. You know that, Cal."

This was tougher than he had expected. Cal wanted to tell the agent where to shove his lousy advances. He wanted to turn on his heel and walk out of this office where they still remembered him as a no-good drunk who couldn't be relied upon to write the captions for a seed catalogue.

He forced himself to remain calm on the surface. "I'm not asking for a hand-out, Lou. I want a job. Something that will pay off right away. I can't work on a novel if my rent's not paid."

The hard lines around Lou's mouth softened. "Yeah," he murmured. He seemed lost in thought for a few minutes. Finally he looked up. "I've got something here you might be interested in. It's a screwy sort of a deal."

"Let's hear it."

"Old gal with lots of loot. She wrote her memoirs for some goddamn reason. Sent them around and all the publishers turned them down. Told her it needs rewriting. She doesn't know rewriting from page eight. Asked me if I would get somebody to do it for her. She's a friend of the family," Lou explained.

Cal waited silently.

"I'll be honest with you. The book's a clinker. It doesn't just need editing, it needs to be written over again. From start to finish. I can't tell her that because her feelings would be hurt. If I can get it published, she won't care what we've done to it."

Lou stopped and stared hard at Cal for a moment. "The way I figure it, if you're half the writer you used to be this job would be a cinch for you. There's lots of good natural material available. Someone who knows how to write could make a pretty good yarn out of it. Think you can handle the job?"

"Maybe. If it's worth it."

Lou laughed. "A minute ago you were dying of malnutrition and now you're gauging the take. I like that." His expression grew serious again. "I can give you five hundred in advance and another five hundred when you finish the job. I figure it should take you about three weeks to do it so I'll expect the completed manuscript on my desk in five. Deal?"

"Deal."

Lou got on the phone and arranged an appointment with the elderly woman. Cal was to ride out to her home on Long Island by train. The chauffeur would pick him up at the station. The interview would be conducted over dinner. Then the procedure would be reversed and Cal would get back to the city late in the evening.

Listening to the way Lou talked to the old dame told him a lot about what to expect. Most of the time Lou just listened. Of the few words he was able to get in edgewise, 90% of them were "Yes, Mrs. Malcolm," or "Of course, Mrs. Malcolm," and What ever you say, Mrs. Malcolm."

A battleax without a doubt. A grade A egoist in the grand tradition with the moola to get her own way. Not altogether an inviting picture of his dinner partner for the evening.

By no means did that mean that Cal wouldn't take the job. Not on your sweet life, sister, he thought. A thousand bucks could keep him going for a quite a while. And Lord knew, he wouldn't sweat for the dough. Lou was allowing him five weeks. From his description of the job, Cal was sure it wouldn't take him that long. Hot as he was now, he probably could knock the job off in a couple of weeks. Five hundred dollars a week was nothing to sneeze at.

"Cal," Lou said as he was about to leave for his appointment, "get to that novel, will you? You're too good to let go to seed."

"I'll write it," Cal promised. "I'm coming on strong, Lou. It won't take me long. Before you know it I'll be coming in here with the best goddamn novel you've read since *Tristram Shandy*."

A rare grin twisted the corners of Lou's lips. Leave it to Cal Staton to guess the book he considered nearer to perfection than anything else he had ever read.

"You can do it, Cal," he said.

Cal left the office feeling great. Really great. Lou had meant that last compliment. He wouldn't throw a bouquet like that around to be polite.

A writer's ego is a shaky thing. Most of the time they're in hell or half way to it. A nice compliment didn't go far with a man who dreamed of being another Tolstoy and produced third-rate Edna Ferber imitations.

Lou's faith in his talent did a great deal for Cal. He felt that he could be just as good as Lou expected him to be.

Someday, Cal thought, maybe Allison will have faith in me too. The thought made an actual physical sensation tingle through his fingers. He yearned for the typewriter.

Mrs. Malcolm turned out to be as obnoxious as he had antic- ipated. He survived the evening by thinking of the thousand bucks. On the way home on the train he skim read her book.

The old bat obviously didn't have the faintest idea of how to write an interesting story. She could take an amusing incident and make it sound as interesting as a lecture on comparative botany. But the difficulties were all stylistic. Fixing the book up would be a cinch. Maybe even polish it off in less than two weeks.

He pulled into Penn Station close to midnight. Twenty-four hours without sleep. He was almost reeling with tiredness. What the hell, with fifty bucks and a check for four hundred and fifty in his pocket, he might as well indulge himself. He hailed a cab.

As Cal settled himself back into the back seat of the cab he recalled how much he had wanted to take a taxi home that very morning. Just fifteen hours ago he had had to walk because his total capital amounted to the magnificent sum of two dollars.

Cal patted the fat bulge his wallet made in his breast pocket and sighed contentedly.

A good night's sleep and tomorrow afternoon he would seek Allison out. He looked forward to telling her of the sudden change in his fortunes.

CHAPTER TEN

Calvin Staton was bugged. Only half way on his search and already his patience was running out. Where the hell did she live?

He hurried on to the next building. And the one after that and the one after that.

There was a basement Italian restaurant on the corner of Greenwich Avenue and Perry Street. The odor of garlic and oregano hit him when he was still several yards away. As he neared the restaurant the smell grew stronger. He wondered idly why they were cooking so early.

Standing directly in front of the building, the overpowering odor enticed him. He glanced at his watch. Almost time for dinner already. No wonder the cooks were busy.

Enticing pictures occurred to him, conjured up by the cooking odors coming from the restaurant. Lasagna, manicotti, veal parmigana, scallopini, shrimps marinara, etc. He realized that he was very hungry.

Small wonder, he reflected. Nothing to eat since the night before. He had hoped Allison would join him in a late lunch. Now here it was already getting on toward dinner time. No wonder his eyes were going cockeyed.

I could almost find my way in there blindfolded, Cal thought, by following the smell. He descended the three steps leading down from street level. Here the path branched. Straight ahead was the entryway to an apartment building. To his right was a door and four more steps that would bring him into the pasta peace of Angelica's.

He turned toward the right. Something held him back. He hadn't checked the apartments above the restaurant. I'll do it later, he thought.

His hand on the restaurant door, he hesitated, then turned and headed back. Oh, what the hell, might as well check the building before eating. It was the last one on that block. After dinner he could start on the other side of the street. Finish all the ones on this side first.

The entryway was small but nice. White tiles set in a hexagonal pattern halfway up and the rest of the walls and the ceiling wallpapered in a tasteful black paper with a delicate silver filigree pattern. He glanced through the thin curtain covering the inside door. Wide marble steps, shiny black banisters and the same wallpaper, this time all the way up from the white baseboard. Converted antique kerosene lamps made of brass and crystal hung at the top and bottom of the staircase, shedding a pleasantly soft light.

Pretty nice for a joint with a spaghetti parlour on the first floor, Cal reflected. But then, the Village was like that. There were swanky buildings all over the Village that looked like ordinary tenements at first glance from the street

He turned to the row of brass mailboxes set into the tile wall. Only five boxes including one for the restaurant, he noted. Each apartment must occupy a whole floor. Very nice. He'd get himself something on that order when he was in better shape financially.

He took his time reading the names on the mailboxes, enjoying the sensation of putting his hunger off. It was delicious just to anticiptae the rich Italian food. A couple minutes longer inhaling the enticing kitchen odors and his appetite would be whetted to just the right point.

No cocktail first, Cal thought. Just a small bottle of good tart Chianti on the table with my meal.

He glanced at the first mailbox. Angelica's. The second mailbox belonged to A. Ciardi. A. Gerald Bassington on the third box. Bernard and Andrea Lehrer got their mail out of the fourth box.

Sharp stabs of hunger like thrusting icicles started hitting Cal in the stomach. He just glanced at the names on the fifth box before turning and heading back toward the restaurant.

Lydia Stone and Allison Fuller. He stopped dead in his tracks. Allison Fuller!?

It couldn't be. He had been searching for that name so long that he must be having hallucinations. He went back to the mailbox.

"Allison Fuller. Sure goddamn 'nough," he muttered aloud. Not even just plain Fuller, another lead that would turn into a disappointment after he had climbed several flights of stairs. Allison Fuller—right out there in plain sight!

Hunger and fatigue vanished instantaneously. He uttered a short prayer that she would be home and pressed the bell. When the buzzer sounded unlocking the downstairs door, he sprinted through and up the four flights of stairs, taking them two steps at a time.

He recognized her voice. He wished that the door were open so that he could see her face when she found out it was he.

Go away? What in blue hell was she raving about? She must think I did something horrible to talk to me this way. He searched his memory.

No, he hadn't done anything wrong. This was ridiculous. If she would only open the door they could discuss their differences like mature adults. Sulking behind a closed door that way was just downright childish.

She still refused to see him. Either she went in big for the dramatic gesture bit or he was missing the point. It just wasn't like her. She had been stoned out of her mind when they met and you can't pretend to be something you're not when you're that high. She had been so warm and helpless and trusting that night. She couldn't have changed this much in three days.

Was she afraid of him? Had he been too forceful with her? Maybe she thought he was some kind of sex maniac who would walk into the apartment, take her clothes off and ravish her on the spot.

He shook his head. It didn't seem likely she'd think anything like that. But he'd try it anyway.

She didn't respond to his promised good behavior. There must be another reason. Why would a girl do something like this? Why not at least let him inside the apartment?

Because there's someone in there with her, he thought. Sure, she lives with that blonde les. Maybe her girl friend found out about the night we spent together and is giving her a hard time. She could be holding Allison prisoner in the apartment. Stranger things have happened.

If she was in trouble he had to help her. Get the police if necessary. Allison was clever. If she couldn't say it right out, she could figure out some way to let him know she needed help.

She said she wasn't in trouble and that he should go away and let her alone.

Cal didn't know what to do. If it was a simple case of not wanting to see him when she was sober, she didn't have to be so theatrical about it. What could be going on behind that closed door?

He stood perfectly still in the silent corridor, too baffled to move.

He heard her fall to the floor. And then the sound of crying. She was sobbing and whispering his name.

Efforts to break the door down got him nowhere. He saw where a new and probably sturdy lock had recently been put on the door. Probably take a tank to bust it down.

She had stopped crying. He tried to talk to her again, find out what was wrong. It was no use. She wouldn't answer him. It was like holding a conversation with the welcome mat.

It was a very long while before he decided that he might as well leave.

The smell of garlic coming from Angelica's repulsed him now. His appetite was gone.

But he was reluctant to leave the vicinity of the building. I'll have a drink at the bar, he decided. He really needed one after that scene upstairs. Besides, standing at Angelica's bar he'd be able to see if anyone came in or out of the building.

He tried to figure it all out over a Scotch and soda. It still didn't make any sense. The only possibility was the suspicion he had had before that her girl friend had come between them.

He was drinking fast, ordering one after another as he tried to imagine what was going on up there.

He should have paid more attention when she told him about being homosexual instead of taking it so lightly. It was because he had known other girls like Allison. Every one he had known had gone through a phase for a while of digging girls and then had gotten over it when they met the right guy.

Maybe Allison was different. Maybe he had only known amateurs before and Allison was a professional. She didn't seem the type. He could have been wrong about her.

Right from the start he had spotted her as mixed-up. She was sick, emotionally warped, mentally ill. So digging girls was just one among her many symptoms.

He had always prided himself on his tolerant understanding of personality quirks and idiosyncrasies. Why should he hold it against Allison if she was a lesbian? He wasn't the sort of man to put a person down just because their sexual preferences were different. If Allison didn't go for men that was her own business. And if she was rejecting him in favor of a girl, at least there was nothing personal in it. He just had the misfortune to go for a girl who didn't go for him.

In which case, Mr. Staton, you just pick up your marbles and go home. You don't keep bothering the nice lady who likes her vice versa.

But did she have to go for Lydia Stone?

There was something about that relationship which prevented Cal from leaving it as it was and bowing out gracefully. He didn't like Lydia. He knew nothing more about her than what he had observed the night of Bill Roman's party and what Allison told him about her later.

No doubt about it, Lydia Stone was a mean bitch. She made life hell for Allison. But would she go so far as to force Allison to keep the door shut in his face? Maybe she would. She was obviously used to getting her own way and didn't give a damn about what happened to anyone else.

A microcephalic idiot would be able to tell that Allison needed professional care. If Lydia was so much in love with the girl why didn't she help her do something about it? She evidently had more than enough cash, certainly enough to pay Allison's fee at a clinic. Why didn't Lydia see to it that Allison got psychiatric help before her illness got worse? The girl was still young, why did Lydia treat her in a manner which would only reinforce her symptoms as the years went on?

Why? Why? Why? Why would Lydia add keeping him and Allison apart to the rest of her sins? Why would Allison chose to stay with a woman who made her so miserable? And why would an intelligent, sophisticated young man like Calvin Staton stand in a bar drinking his fool head off and risking all the hard won equilibrium it had taken him months to regain and a fat, juicy editing assignment that would keep him in typewriter ribbons for a long time to come and put him back in the good graces of the best literary agent in New York City just because he had met a good-looking girl at a party who had appealed to him and who had slept with him for all of one night? For one lousy night!!!

Cal put his half finished drink down on the bar and signalled to the bartender for his check. He had been leaning on the bar, his chin in his hand, one foot hooked around the rail. He stepped backward one step for more room in which to put his overcoat on.

He couldn't stop! His feet kept making the backward step!

Luckily, there was a broad pillar a few feet behind where he had been standing. His backward movement was halted by it. The impact of the solid shaft against his back made his head snap forward with a nerve-twinging crack.

He kept his back firmly aligned against the pillar until the dizziness passed. Whew! He had no idea he had drunk that much.

See what can happen? he scolded himself as if he were a willful child. That's what knocking yourself out over a woman does to you. If you keep chasing after that goddamn lesbian you'll end up right back on skid row.

Not me. Not anymore. I've learned my lesson. No woman will ever mean that much to me again.

He managed to get to a nearby luncheonette without incident. There he ate a light, healthy dinner. From the luncheonette he headed toward Washington Square Park. Object: to keep walking around the Park until the fresh air and food cleared his head.

An hour later Cal Staton was taking a hot bath in the Cornelia Street apartment house where he lived. A cold shower, deep breaths of frosty air at the open window and he was back to normal.

He sat down at his desk, placed the manuscript to his right and a ream of bond paper to the left of the typewriter. He would work until he fell asleep from exhaustion and get back to work as soon as he woke up. Work was the only way he knew to keep away from the two things that terrified him—liquor and wanting Allison.

He couldn't write creatively when he was emotionally upset but working at the rewrite desk of a hick newspaper for a year had taught him how to throw himself into that job so completely everything else was blocked out. He could make editorial corrections on his own obituary without turning a hair.

He turned the desk lamp on, rolled a sheet of paper into the typewriter and lit a cigarette. "Goodbye, Allison," he whispered as his fingers poised in readiness above the typewriter keys.

CHAPTER ELEVEN

Lydia had been in jail for over a week. Paul Spencer was doing everything he could to get her out but it looked as if she'd have to stay in prison another week or so at least.

Allison visited her for half an hour five times a week. If the rules allowed it, she would have spent even more time there. Indeed, if it were only possible, she would gladly serve Lydia's jail sentence for her.

The Women's House of Detention was no place for someone like Lydia. She hated rules and regulations. Her whole life had been spent in pursuit of excitement and kicks. It was hell for her being locked up with a pack of dull-witted streetwalkers and petty thieves.

Lydia was looking better, Allison thought. Ever since she had been in prison, Lydia had been neglecting her appearance. This afternoon her hair was neatly combed and she had put on a little makeup.

She looks more cheerful too. Allison wondered why the sullen expression which had been clouding Lydia's face was gone.

They chatted and laughed together pleasantly. God, what a relief seeing Lydia acting like herself again!

Toward the end of the visiting period a young girl walked near. Lydia's face lit up when she saw her. "Anne," she called. "Anne, come over here. There's someone I want you to meet."

The girl turned at the sound of her own name being called. She walked toward them slowly. She came to a halt alongside Lydia.

Lydia looked up at Anne and smiled. Anne smiled, slowly and crookedly like an embarrassed adolescent boy. They looked deep into each others eyes, knowing nothing else in that moment.

Lydia shivered as if forcing herself out of a trance and brought her attention back to Allison. "Anne Spengler," she explained, "My new cell-mate. She just came in yesterday."

Visiting time was over. Guards was shooing the visitors out.

"What a shame," Lydia said as she was leaving. "I had hoped you two would have more time to get acquainted."

Of all the damn times for the visiting period to end! Allison forced herself to walk calmly out of the jail. While all the time she was raging inside.

She wanted to kick, scream, yell, throw furniture, break windows. What right had these guards with their stupid rules and regulations to make her leave at a time like this? Just when her whole life was being taken away from her back there inside the prison! And she was helpless because she couldn't do anything about it. She couldn't stop them when she had to go away this way and leave them alone together. And she could hardly risk getting herself arrested. With her luck they'd lock her up in another part of the prison altogether.

Meet Anne. She's sharing a cell with me. What was I supposed to say, Allison thought bitterly. Should I have said, "How nice. You must invite me to your housewarming."?

No wonder Lydia was so chipper today! Nothing to make the old girl bubble like a nice new play-mate.

Allison had no doubts about Anne. One look at Lydia's new friend and she had the whole picture. Anne was young, in her late teens or early twenties at most. She was short and stocky, her compact body hard and muscled like an athlete's. Her coarse hair was bleached almost white, worn brushed flat along the sides and cut in a D. A. in back. Most men wore their hair longer than Anne did.

Her young face was almost expressionless. The blank appearance that comes from experiencing too much too soon and not liking most of it. The stiffly controlled muscles of Anne's face betrayed a girl so beaten down by life that only two emotions remained alive in her—desire and anger when frustrated.

A typical picture. Anne was cut from the same mold as most of the young dykes who hung around the Village bars. The mindless, heartless mass of lost young women who live only for the embrace of another woman and who support themselves by running errands for small-time criminals.

This was what Lydia was carrying on with. Allison knew that even in jail there are ways to get enough privacy. Lydia could charm the stripes off a tiger when she put her mind to it. It would be an easy matter for her to talk a guard into turning her back for an hour or so.

So Lydia had replaced her. All the months they had lived together, the love they had shared, meant no more to her than this—a woman—a woman who would be Lydia's own—to share her bed. She had never cared for Allison any more than she would for any female who would willingly submit.

If only Lydia had told her, prepared her for Anne somehow. That would be different. There had been plenty of other women before, women Lydia had brought home for both of them to enjoy. She had even encouraged Allison to pick up women, telling her always to "bring them home to Mama".

This time Lydia had found a play-mate for herself exclusively. An uncouth diesel dyke who probably never took a bath unless she was forced into it.

Allison was mad. More than that, she was hurt. Anne's appearance on the scene made all that she had shared with Lydia meaningless. The "Great Love" had actually been nothing more than a matter of convenience to Lydia. All the great understanding and tender concern Lydia had shown—that had been nothing more than a way of binding Allison closer. She had been a useful servant, paid in wages of false love.

She wasn't going to take this lying down. Lydia wasn't going to get away with flaunting her lovers in front of her face that way! She'd show Lydia she couldn't be pushed around. She'd hit back and hurt Lydia as the older woman had hurt her. And she knew just how to go about it—Cal Staton!

She was at his place on Cornelia Street within a few minutes. Up the stairs and in front of the door to his apartment. Behind her, in the bathroom, a girl stood combing her hair. The girl was only wearing a bra and panties yet she had the door to the bathroom wide open and looked as unconcerned as if she were fully clothed. The girl stared at Allison openly, not attempting to hide the slightly hostile curiosity in her eyes.

Allison knocked on the door to Cal's apartment.

There was no answer.

She knocked again.

Allison rapped on Cal's door one more time.

"I don't think he's home, honey," the girl in the bathroom called out to her.

"Oh? Do you know when he'll be back?"

"Nope. You a friend of his?" the girl asked.

"Uh, yes. That is—could you give him a message for me?"

"Sure."

"I mean—will you be seeing him soon?"

"Sure. I live here. I see him all the time. My name's Nancy."

"I'm Allison Fuller. Will you tell Cal that I came by to see him?"

"Sure. Tough—his not being home, I mean. After you climbed all those steps and all."

Allison didn't like the look in Nancy's eyes. She had seen that look before. The taunting look that some straight women get when they meet a lesbian. The look that challenges, that says, "try and make me."

"I appreciate your giving Cal my message. Good night," Allison said stiffly.

"See you around sometime, honey," Nancy called after her as she ran down the stairs.

Allison didn't know what she felt like doing. All she knew was what she didn't want to do. She didn't want to go back to the apartment and be the good little repentant sinner. That bit had ended the minute Anne appeared on the scene.

She wandered aimlessly around the Village for a while. It was cold and gradually the chill crept through her clothes. She couldn't stay out in the open much longer. Besides, she was thirsty. A coke would have satisfied her thirst but her mood demanded liquor. The raw, burning, smoky taste of sin.

She cut through Washington Square Park and up Thompson Street. Down a flight of stairs and past a man with a smashed-up face who looked her over carefully.

Nice to be recognized, Allison thought. Even in a place like the Harbor where the only people who couldn't get in were those who preferred their sex with a member of the opposite sex. It had been months since the last time she had come here with Lydia but the bouncer remembered her. She was accepted as a member of the most non-exclusive club in the world.

It wasn't very crowded. Too early, Allison thought. I should have come in later. But she didn't feel up to going out into the cold night again.

No one there she knew. That was good. No one who would ask her about Lydia and make her invent excuses for being out alone.

Allison knew the routine down to a T. She found a seat at the end of the bar near the door where she could see everyone in the place and be seen by them. Instead of giving her coat to the hatcheck girl, she draped it casually across her shoulders. That way she looked as if she might get up and leave at any moment, as if she was alone and not waiting for someone to join her.

Never letting her gaze wander from the bartender's face, she ordered a drink. Scotch with water on the side. She paid for it with a five dollar bill and let the change remain on the counter. Only when she had raised the glass of liquor to her lips did she allow her eyes to wander down the length of the bar.

Two of them, she registered silently to herself. Two butches on the loose. Both of them with their elbows on the bar, leaning hunched over their beers. Both of them looking for a pick-up.

Allison made a quick bet with herself that the short one wearing the open-necked lumber shirt would approach her first.

I'm attractive, she reassured herself. I appeal to women.

She reached into her pocketbook and brought out a pack of cigarettes. Deliberately, she fumbled getting the cigarette out of the pack, creating the impression that she wasn't accustomed to handling such difficult matters herself.

Finding a match was an even more demanding task. Allison groped around in her bag for several minutes. There were two packs of matches and a cigarette lighter in there. She felt them but she'd be damned if she would let anyone else know she did.

Smell of burning sulphur and a flame inches before her eyes.

It had worked! Allison bent forward, lighting her cigarette on the proferred match.

"My name is Sandy. What's yours, honey?"

The rest of it had been right out of the rule books. A cinch. Allison congratulated herself on her professional technique. Sandy had said the usual nonsense and she had responded in kind. They had talked about everything and nothing. And they had had a couple of drinks and smiled at each other a few times as if they really meant it.

And now here they were. Just like that! Somehow it had all happened with the unthinking ease of a ritual. There had been an easily managed beginning and they had taken it from there like two actors reading a script. Somewhere along the line Allison had agreed to accompany Sandy home. And now she was alone with Sandy in Sandy's apartment. Nothing could be simpler.

Lydia plays with Anne, Allison plays with Sandy. Really, life was very simple.

Allison got up from the chair where she had been sitting. She didn't feel like relaxing here, that wasn't what she had come for. She walked around the tiny living room impatiently waiting for Sandy to come back from the kitchen where she was getting ice for their drinks.

Sandy came in with a mixing bowl full of ice cubes. She carried it over to the low cocktail table in front of the couch, sat down and fixed drinks for both of them.

Allison sat down at the other end of the couch. She accepted her drink soundlessly. Since they had entered the apartment neither of them had said a word.

They sat in silence for a few minutes longer. Allison didn't feel uncomfortable. More than anything else, she was bored by Sandy's silence.

She raised the glass to her lips and sipped. Too strong, hardly any water in it at all. She put it carefully back down on the cocktail table.

"You don't like your drink?" Sandy asked.

"It's O.K.," Allison lied. "I just don't feel like drinking any more tonight."

Sandy placed her drink alongside Allison's. She remained bent over the cocktail table, her face averted. "What do you feel like?" she asked in a husky whisper.

"Don't you know?"

Sandy looked up at her. Her lips were drawn in a tight smile. There was a devilish light in her eyes. "No. Tell me about it."

Allison was irritated. What kind of nonsense was Sandy pulling? All right, so they had to talk to each other. That was part of the game. You talked for a few minutes and convinced yourself and the other person that you weren't just an animal and then you got down to business. That much she was prepared to put up with. But Sandy was making it difficult, playing coy. Who the hell did she think she was fooling?

She made her voice soft and suggestive. "I don't know, Sandy. I get the feeling I don't really have to tell you anything. I think you know already."

Sandy leaned back on the couch. She lit a cigarette and blew smoke toward the ceiling, her whole manner expressing unconcern.

A blinding fury swept through Allison. She didn't have to take this sort of nonsense. Not from Sandy, anyway. Who the hell did she think she was? She wouldn't be so damned cocky if she knew I was just using her to hit back at Lydia.

Was that entirely true? Allison was too honest to completely believe the lie she had been telling herself all night. No, there was more to it. She had to be with Sandy tonight. She had to feel someone's arms around her. Know that a woman cared, if only for as long as her body thirsted.

"Why did you ask me to come with you, Sandy?"

Sandy laughed. "Now who's asking the questions?"

"Don't make me beg, Sandy." Hot anger made Allison clip the end off each word. "Please, don't make me beg."

Sandy grabbed her shoulders and drew her close. They kissed.

Sandy broke away. "Are you sure you want me?" she asked.

"Sandy, will you stop all these stupid questions?"

"No. I've got to know. I'm not the kind who likes to force a girl."

Allison was touched by the girl's pathetic need. It was so transparent, so childish. And yet, if that's what Sandy wanted, she'd give it to her. If Sandy needed to delude herself each time she went to bed with a girl, that was her own business.

"I want you very much, Sandy. I—I like you very much." Allison cursed herself. If she was going to lie, why couldn't she have lied all the way? It would have meant so much to Sandy if she had said she loved her.

Apparently she had said enough. The anxiety went out of Sandy's face. In its stead came a look of naked lust. "Oh, baby," she breathed.

They stood up. Sandy watched hungrily while Allison slowly stripped all her clothes off. She studied Allison's body with open admiration.

Allison had to restrain herself from running away Sandy made her feel uncomfortable. As if she were deliberately teasing her.

Oh Lord, what was Sandy waiting for? Why did she have to act like every other lesbian, needing to dominate, to reduce the other girl to a state of humiliation?

What was she doing here? What was it all for? Why prove to herself that Sandy could do this to her? Briefly Allison thought to herself that she might as well forget the whole thing and go back to Lydia. Lydia who hurt and tormented her—but so would any other woman.

No, Lydia had gone too far. Allison had to sleep with Sandy tonight if only because Lydia was with Anne.

Sandy placed her palms against Allison's cheeks. "You're very beautiful, you know. I could really go for you."

Allison couldn't repress a shudder of revulsion. Sandy had looked at hundreds of women in just this way and said the same words to them. It meant nothing. Less than nothing.

Simulating faintness, Allison collapsed backward onto the couch. Sandy was beside her instantly, her stubby tobacco-stained fingers on her breasts.

Allison looked down at her own body. She saw the sensitive tissues responding to Sandy's manipulating fingers, but inside herself Allison felt nothing. Her body responded automatically, while all the time all she could think of was how silly they would both look to an observer.

"What's the matter, baby? Don't you like what I'm doing?"

"I ..." Allison didn't get a chance to answer. Sandy's mouth came down on hers in a kiss that bruised her lips.

Confident with the technique that had aroused countless other women, Sandy sought to awaken Allison's body. She nipped the tender breasts.

It hurt. Allison realized with surprise that was all she felt. With Lydia the pain had always been mixed with pleasure. This time nothing aroused her. It was all silly and a little irritating.

What had happened to her? Why couldn't she respond? What did she want?

Unwanted, unbidden, the answer came to her. Calvin Staton.

She wanted his strong arms around her. His lips on hers. Cal came to her clean, a man seeking to give and receive pleasure with a woman.

This—this playing games with a woman she didn't know and felt no affection for—this was no answer to anything.

Allison felt pity for Sandy stir deep within her. Sandy was knocking herself out and no matter what she did Allison just wasn't going to respond. She would have if she could. But it was impossible. Her body was shut off from Sandy as if there were a brick wall around it.

But Sandy was lost and unhappy just as she herself was. It would be too cruel to hurt her more than she had been hurt already. Allison thought of a solution.

Allison braced her foot against the floor, tensed all her muscles, wrapped her arms around the other girl's back and, with a tremendous surge of strength, flipped them both over. She collapsed, panting for breath.

"Hey, what the hell ... ?" Sandy asked, thoroughly baffled.

"Tonight I want to be Daddy," Allison answered.

"Aw, but ..."

"Shut up."

Allison unfastened Sandy's shirt. She didn't bother reaching in back to undo her bra. Instead, she grabbed the front of it and ripped it free.

Sandy had been hiding a very nice, thoroughly feminine body under all those truck driver's clothes. Allison appreciated that, it made her task a lot easier.

Allison came on hard and fast. Her lips on Sandy's breast, she kneaded the soft flesh of her thighs in her hand.

"Oh-h-h," Sandy breathed.

Allison congratulated herself. She had guessed correctly. Like so many other butches, Sandy loved to get on her back once in a while.

CHAPTER TWELVE

Allison practically lived with Sandy for the next week. Her life consisted of trips to the jail to see Lydia and be tormented by the ever-present Anne, stop-overs at the apartment to walk and feed Prufrock and back to Sandy.

It was horrible, degrading. Sandy was nothing to her. A bore. A silly, sentimental, witless girl who only knew how to do one thing. And it was precisely that one thing which kept drawing Allison back.

She hated Sandy. Not because the girl had done anything to her but because of the power she had over her. The power to make Allison keep coming back, humble and humiliated.

There was desire in Sandy's arms. Desire and passion and ecstasy.

There was nothing else in Allison's life. The present was horrible and the future loomed even grimmer. Lydia had replaced her with Anne. Sure, Lydia would be getting out of jail soon. But that didn't mean everything would be the same again. If Lydia could get involved with Anne then Allison had to face the possibility of other women who might come between them.

There was another angle too. Allison realized that going to the jail to visit Lydia was becoming a chore. She didn't look forward to seeing Lydia any more. When they were together, Allison was irritated by Lydia's constant critical attitude and her bossiness.

She didn't even feel very jealous of Anne. More than any-thing else she felt disappointed in Lydia that she would become involved with such a stupid girl.

The conclusion was inescapable. Allison admitted to herself that her love for Lydia was lessening with each passing day.

There was no middle ground with Lydia. One could either love her or hate her. Allison knew that they could never live together again. Lydia was hardly the sort of woman anyone could live with as a casual friend.

But without Lydia—what? Life had been hell before Lydia and life would be hell after her. There was nothing left to look forward to except—except the person who had come between them—the man who had made her feel as no other man ever had—Calvin Staton.

Allison ran to Cal as a bird will fly to shelter from a storm. Only there was no shelter with Cal. She came after him time and again, humbling herself. He was never there when she needed him.

All the times she stopped at his apartment, she found the door locked tight and no answer when she knocked. Her mes-sages went unanswered.

There was only one conclusion to be drawn—Cal didn't want to see her, to have anything to do with her. The time when she had refused to let him in had spelled the end of their relationship.

No Lydia, no Cal, no future. Today was a nightmare and tomorrow would be worse. Allison sought oblivion in Sandy's arms.

Cal Staton finished Mrs. Malcolm's "autobiography" sooner than he had expected to. By throwing himself single-mindedly into the effort, he managed to get it done in a little over a week.

Lou Stotz read it and liked it. Mrs. Malcolm approved of the changes he had made. The deal was completed all around. Cal left Lou's office with the final five hundred dollar payment in his pocket.

That gave him, after he had paid off most of his debts, a neat seven hundred dollars to his credit. Enough to live on for several months. Enough to get him more than started on the novel.

The publisher who had brought out his last book was anxious to get hold of the new one. Lou was so hungry for it it was pathetic. Cal was so bursting with enthusiasm he could hardly wait to get back to work.

Editing someone else's manuscript and creative writing are two entirely different things, requiring entirely different states of mind. Cal had been able to suspend himself above his emotions while he worked on Mrs. Malcolm's book. When he tried to start his own novel, he just couldn't make it.

There's only one thing a creative writer can write about—himself. He may write about people entirely different from himself, places he's never been, things he has never done. It doesn't matter. The only way he can know what to write about is by imagining how he would react to the situations he puts his characters in. A writer has to be in touch with himself.

Cal ripped up nine pages for every ten he wrote. The one he kept wasn't much good either. The novel wasn't going badly—it just plain wasn't going.

The reason was obvious to him. He didn't want to write. His body and mind were exhausted from working on Mrs. Malcolm's script.

That was only a fraction of the story. The real truth was that he couldn't write because something else was on his mind. Because the memory of something beautiful and precious made everything else seem useless. Because he thought of Allison constantly.

Allison didn't want him. She had made that perfectly clear. He could write if he had Allison. And since he couldn't have her, there was only one thing to do. Forget her. Forget her so he could clear his mind for writing.

So he carefully put the cover on his typewriter and went out and got drunk.

Cal sat in the bar drinking and loving Allison. It wasn't the first time he had been in love. His dead wife had been more precious to him than anything else on earth. She was gone now though and nothing would bring her back.

The way Cal felt toward Allison was different. His love for his wife had been filled with youthful exuberance and optimism. Cal loved Allison as only a man who has suffered can love. He loved her as much for her beauty and youth as for her need for him.

But what kind of a girl had he fallen in love with? A girl who was a lesbian. Who preferred a woman to him. A girl who had let him hold her in his arms only once. A girl he could never marry.

She might break up with Lydia. Big lot of good that would do him. Once a lesbian always a lesbian. She'd latch on to some other woman. And then where would he be? Thrown over for a dyke.

It was really very funny if you looked at it in the right way. Very funny. Hilarious. Cal felt like laughing so much tears came to his eyes.

The other people in the dimly lit bar turned to look at the man laughing and crying at the same time. Cal saw them watching him and pulled himself together. No use making a fool of himself. Everybody's got troubles.

Troubles like his? Troubles like falling in love with a lesbian? Could be. Anything was possible. Particularly if your name was Cal Staton and you had two talents in life: writing and getting mixed up with the wrong women.

He ordered another drink. It was good to be able to tell the bartender to bring another Scotch and water. Just like other people did. And it was nice to be in a place where he could be alone with his thoughts even though he was surrounded by people.

Cal was in a run-down longshoremen's bar down near the river. He chose the place because he had come in there with Harry a few times. Being in a familiar bar with a bartender who minded his own business was just what the doctor ordered.

The "Scotch" was bottled across the river and came from a distillery two states away. It was carmel-flavored poison but Cal didn't mind. He was out to get drunk, not to waste his hard earned capital and the rotgut came at half a dollar a shot. It had been aged about three days but a man could get just as blotto on it as he could on the stuff that was stamped *by appointment to the Queen.*

Cal fished in his pocket. Empty. He tried his other pocket. Two dimes and a quarter. Sweat broke out on his forehead.

Then he remembered the ten folded inside his key case. He breathed a deep sigh of relief and signalled to the barkeep for another shot.

How much money had he started out with? How many drinks had he had so far? He couldn't remember. And when the bartender put the shot glass down in front of him and didn't bother giving him a glass of water, he tried and couldn't remember when he had stopped using a chaser.

He looked at his reflection in the mirror over the bar. I don't like my face, he decided. I don't like it one bit.

Below the bar mirror were shelves of liquor bottles. Cal searched among them for the brand he was drinking. He saw it. Allison Fuller Scotch the label read.

Something wrong there. Cal decided that what was wrong was that he hadn't had enough to drink yet.

He wanted to be drunk, stoned, four sheets to the wind, blotto. What was the use of staying sober? Being sober meant remembering. Remembering two women. One of them dead and the other one unavailable. Calvin Staton could see no point at all in remaining sober.

Someone sat down on the stool next to him. "Hello, Cal," the blur beside him said in a familiar voice.

"Hello, Harry."

"Mind if I join you?"

"Free country. Got time for a drink?"

"Yeah. Don't have to get to work for another hour."

"I'll join you then." Cal called the bartender over and ordered double Scotches for himself and Harry.

"You've had a couple," Harry commented.

"I've had more than a couple. Tell him how many I've had," Cal instructed the bartender.

The bartender mumbled something to Harry.

Harry turned toward Cal, a disapproving frown on his ugly face. "What for you drinking like this? You out to be bum all your life? Don't you ever learn a lesson?"

"I, my dear Harold, have learned a very good lesson. This," Cal raised his shot glass, "is my graduation exercise."

Harry snorted in disgust. "What lesson you learn?"

"I have learned," Cal spoke with drunken precision, "that I am very much in love and I can't live without the woman I love."

"Hey, that's great. Tell you what, why don't you bring your girl up to my place for supper some night? My wife would love to meet her."

Cal raised the shot glass to eye level and stared into it thoughtfully. "Does your wife love lesbians, Harry?"

"What the hell you getting at?" Harry's hand tightened into a fist then relaxed as he got the idea. "Oh, you in love with a dyke?"

"Yeah. Ain't it a bitch?"

"It's a bitch," Harry agreed. "Not much a man can do when he's in love with a lesbian."

"Not much," Cal echoed.

"Except drink," Harry added.

"Nothing else he can do."

"This one's on me." Harry signalled the barkeep to bring two more doubles.

The bartender brought the drinks and leaned across the bar to speak to Harry. "What's with your friend?" he asked.

"In love with a lesbian," Harry answered.

"That true?" the bartender asked Cal.

"Couldn't be truer."

The bartender reached beneath the bar and brought up a bottle of genuine Chivas Regal. He set up three glasses, for Cal, Harry and himself. "This one's on the house," he said.

Allison ran up the four flights of steps. She was late. Damn Sandy for getting amorous at the wrong times! She would just have time to run Prufrock once around the block before she was due at the jail to see Lydia.

She put her key in the lock and started to turn it. The door swung open.

"I was wondering when you'd finally decide to come home."

Lydia was standing in the doorway! Lydia, looking angry and impatient as if she had been waiting there for hours.

"When … ?"

"When did I get out of jail? Last night. Paul finally managed my release. Don't just stand there. Come inside."

Allison followed Lydia into the apartment. She was dazed, in a state of shock. Lydia had been home since last night. She had been waiting for Allison.

Lydia controlled her anger with great effort. Only the white edge around her nostrils betrayed her fury. "Where were you last night?" she demanded.

"I—I was with a friend."

"Who?"

"You don't know her." Allison searched her mind for a name to give her. She couldn't think of anyone. It didn't matter. Lydia would sense the truth anyway.

"You were with another woman!" Lydia screamed.

Allison didn't answer.

"Admit it! You might as well tell me because I know already. Admit you were with another woman! Tell me all about it, Allison. I want to know everything you did and said with her."

No answer.

Lydia drew her arm far back. The swing came from the shoulder, her palm hitting Allison's cheek with all the force she could put behind it. "Tell me everything," Lydia hissed.

The blow sent Allison reeling. She hit the wall and slid to the floor. For a few seconds all she was aware of was a sound that was like high-pitched humming inside her head. Flashes of brilliantly colored light flickered before her eyes.

Then her head cleared. Lydia was standing in front of her, hands on her hips, face twisted with rage. Sprawled on the floor, sobbing and gulping for air, blood trickling down on her clothes from her split lip, Allison told her about Sandy.

When she was through, there was a strained silence for several minutes. Then Lydia knelt down and grasped her hands and helped her to her feet.

Lydia's eyes were strangely dilated. Her lips were drawn back against her teeth in a grotesque smile. "You're so bad, Allison. The minute I turn my back you do bad things to hurt me. Isn't that right, Allison?"

Allison nodded, keeping her eyes averted.

"You know what happens when you're bad. Mommy has to punish you so you won't be bad again."

"Yes," Allison breathed.

"Lie down on the bed."

Allison walked into the bedroom and lay face down on the bed. She was numb with despair.

Lydia was gone for a few minutes. When she returned Allison looked up and saw that she had a thick leather belt in her hands. Allison turned her head back down into the pillow and bit the cover between her teeth.

"Lie still," Lydia commanded.

Allison felt cool air against her thighs as Lydia pulled her skirt up around her waist. Then she arched her back to help Lydia as she tugged her panties off.

The stinging lash of the belt against her bare backside made Allison jump.

"Lie still, I told you," Lydia hissed. She raised the belt again.

Allison hurt. Her body was aching all over from the places where the belt had hit. Especially her behind. That was raw with pain.

She pressed her face deeper into the pillow and tried to stifle her screams.

"Oh God, this is beautiful," Lydia gasped from low in her throat. "Oh Allison, Allison. Tell me that my bad little girl loves her Mommy."

Allison raised her head and looked at Lydia. She opened her mouth to say the words.

They wouldn't come! She struggled, gasping through her tears. Why couldn't she say it? Why couldn't her lips form the words I love you? She fought against herself but no words would come out.

Lydia's face went white with anger. Her whole body shook with the force of her rage. She grasped the other end of the belt and swung it behind her. The metal buckle came down on Allison's back, cutting deep into the raw blisters.

Allison screamed and writhed as the buckle slashed her again and again. This wasn't fair! This was going too far!

Yes, she had been bad. And yes she deserved to be punished by Lydia. But Lydia was hurting her too much.

The spankings and all the rest she could understand. Even the times before when Lydia had hit her with the belt, she hadn't really minded it because she knew she deserved to be punished.

But the metal buckle! That was too much. That was worse punishment than anyone could deserve.

She heard the belt drop to the floor. Then Lydia was lying on the bed beside her.

Lydia nuzzled her lips against Allison's neck. She was trembling with passion. Her hands caressed the tender flesh of Allison's back. "I love my little girl," Lydia crooned. "See how much I love you?" She dug her sharp nails into the raw flesh of Allison's behind.

Allison screamed. She tore herself away from Lydia. She sprang to her feet and stood uncertainly beside the bed for a moment, waiting for the floor to stop rocking.

Lydia was coming after her! Lydia was inching across the bed in her direction, her eyes glowing like blue fire!

Allison grabbed the clock-radio off the bedstand. She held it high in both hands. "You're not my mother!" she shouted as she brought the radio down with all her might on the back of Lydia's head.

CHAPTER THIRTEEN

The first thing he was conscious of was light. Bright, glaring lights that were searing through his eyelids.

Next, he felt himself shivering. That came first and then the sensation of cold.

Cal opened his eyes and looked around him. Christ, no wonder he was cold! He was lying in a corner of the loading platform with only his overcoat over him.

"Glad to see you're still alive."

He blinked his eyes several times before the dark shape would come into focus. Finally he made out his friend Harry squatting beside him.

"Hello, Harry," Cal said weakly.

"Hello, dope." Harry grinned.

"Should I ask how I got here?"

"Simple. You decided to get some fresh air so you walked to work with me. You were very, very drunk, my friend. I carried you the last block."

"Oh."

"How do you feel?"

Cal thought about that. He decided that he felt like hell warmed over. His mouth was so dry his tongue stuck to the roof of his mouth. There was a big balloon full of air in the middle of his guts and a throbbing pain in his skull that felt as if it was pushing the lid off.

"I feel o.k.," he told Harry.

"I'll bet. Here, take some of this. It'll make you feel better."

Cal took the bottle in his hand and lowered it to his lips. The smell of the stuff made him gag. He concentrated hard on numbing all his senses for a second. If he could get a couple of swallows down and hold them there, he'd be all right in a few minutes.

He tilted the bottle. It was like pouring liquid fire down his throat.

Harry grabbed the bottle from his shaking hands. He waited until the spasm passed then pressed the bottle against Cal's lips again and held it until Cal swallowed another mouthful.

That one went down easier. In fact, it felt good. Sensation began to come back.

Cal pulled himself to his feet. Luckily, there was a barrel against the wall. He made it over to the barrel and seated himself on it just before his knees gave out.

"You'll be o.k. Just take it easy for a little while. I'll be back in a coupla minutes," Harry said.

Cal sat on the barrel. Harry had been right. As the liquor did its job he began to feel like something remotely resembling a human being again.

"Here, eat this," Harry shoved a container of coffee and a Danish pastry toward him.

Cal did as he was told. Harry stood watching him with a cynical smile. The smile didn't hide the anxious look in his eyes.

He's like a mother hen, Cal thought as he munched on the pastry. How could someone so ugly be so nice? It's like having an ape for a nursemaid. A warm rush of affection for Harry flooded through Cal. Best goddamn ape in the whole world, he thought. Smartest, nicest, best goddamn ape there is.

"Guess you better go home and take a bath now."

Cal looked down at himself. His clothes were a mess. Dirty, ripped, encrusted with grime.

He got up and grinned at Harry. That was all. The big man would understand. If Cal tried to thank him, he'd be insulted and if he dared to tell Harry how much he liked him, Harry would probably pick him up by the seat of his pants and throw him off the platform.

"Say hello to your girl for me," Harry called after him.

Cal turned and walked back. "What girl?"

"The one you were talking about when you was tanked last night."

"Allison?"

"Yeah, that was her name."

"Did I say much about her, Harry?"

"You was telling me your troubles."

Cal stared at the platform. "She's a lesbian, Harry."

"Yeah, I know. You told me about her. While you were sleeping it off, I been thinking about what you said. It don't make no difference."

"What do you mean?"

"You go for her and she goes for you. It don't make any difference she's a lesbian." Harry shuffled his feet uncomfortably. It was hard for him to say what he felt he had to. "You take my wife now. She had tuberculosis before I married her. I knew about it. The way I figured it, she was all alone and so was I. I could beat my brains out because she was sick and I wanted to marry her. And she could just go on feeling sorry for herself because she was sick and nobody gave a damn. So I married her and I did what I could for her. You know, doctors, sanitariums, all that. She's o.k. now. And she don't forget that I didn't walk out on her when she needed me."

"It's not the same, Harry."

"It never is."

Cal headed east through the quiet streets of the Village. He liked walking around the Village at that time when the people were all off the streets and the early dawn cast a flattering pale lemon light on the neat buildings.

This morning he didn't see much as he walked along. His head was too full of what Harry had said. Harry's story wasn't relevant to his own, of course. But he couldn't stop thinking about it and carrying on an argument with the other man in his mind.

Harry just doesn't understand, Cal thought. He's a nice simple guy who sees everything in black and white. He can't understand a problem like mine.

Now, Harry's problem was very simple. He was in love with a girl who had an illness. Her body was sick. Doctors know how to cure tuberculosis. What Harry's girl needed was someone who gave a damn about her who would help her get the treatment she needed. So Harry married her and sent her to the right doctors and she got well again. It isn't the same thing at all.

From the back of his brain a voice remarkably like that of a crotchety fossil of an Ancient History professor Cal had had in college asked a question. "Will someone please give the class a definition of homosexuality?" the voice asked.

"Homosexuality is a symptom of mental illness," Cal recited to the imaginary professor.

"And can it be cured?"

"Yes. In most cases, with the help of a trained therapist, if the patient sincerely desires to change his or her sexual pattern, a cure is quite possible."

Cal stopped walking. He swayed against a building and pressed his forehead to the cool wooden doorframe.

Oh Christ, forgive me. Cal was glad there was no one around to see him leaning against the building and see the hot tears that splashed down his face.

I'm no good and I'll never be any good because all I can think of is myself. Give me, give me—just like a baby. If I don't get what I want I throw a tantrum and run away.

Drinking—what the hell was that for? I was just feeling sorry for myself again.

What have I got to feel sorry for?

I can take care of myself. I'm healthy and strong and talented. The world's my oyster if I'd just take the trouble to open the shell.

Allison—she's the one who needs sympathy, not me. She's lost and confused and sick. Yeah, sick—just like Harry's wife. Only Harry's an all right guy. He wouldn't walk out on someone he loved just because everything wasn't champagne and roses right from the start.

So she told me to go away. Then she came by and left messages with Nancy. And I told myself she was just playing games with me. Oh Allison, forgive me! I should have known.

Maybe she's in trouble. She's all alone in the world with only that Lydia creep to turn to. And that dame is in even worse shape than Allison. God only knows what goes on between those two.

Allison needs me. She needs me desperately. I say that I'm in love with her but what do I do? I walk out on her.

Cal wiped his eyes on the back of his sleeve. He looked up at the sky. The rim of the sun was just visible above the tops of the warehouses along Hudson Street.

I've got to go to her, Cal addressed the orange ball in the sky. I've got to help her because I need her as much as she needs me. She's all wrong inside now but I'll help make her all right. And when she's happy, I'll be happy too.

He walked rapidly toward Greenwich Avenue. If I never write another word again it'll be all right, he told the sun. But if I do write, I'll write the best goddamn books in the world because of Allison.

Allison came out of the long night of unconsciousness slowly. As the sights, sounds and smells around her began to make sense, she struggled to remember what had happened.

One thing was sure—she had had another one of her headaches. This one must have been a whopper. Why else would there be a doctor bending over her, holding a stethescope to her chest?

There was a woman sitting in a chair near the bed. The woman was wearing some kind of funny looking white hat.

Lydia!

Allison sat up abruptly, almost colliding with the doctor. As she moved, hot stabs of pain shot up and down her back. She gasped involuntarily and placed her hands tentatively on the place where it hurt.

Behind the doctor's back, Lydia gestured frantically. Allison got the message. Lydia was signalling her to try and keep the doctor from seeing her lacerated behind.

The whole chain of memory was set off. The doctor was saying something to her but all she heard was that he was leaving her a prescription for tranquilizers. She ignored the rest of his assurances that she would be all right after a little rest.

Allison was thinking of more important matters. She was remembering the previous night. Suppose she had killed Lydia? Well, no use thinking of that. That was obviously no ghost sitting in the chair.

She pressed her lips together to keep back the giggle. Lydia really did look awfully funny in that bandage. Allison knew she ought to be feeling contrite. She tried to feel guilty. It was no use. All she could feel was silly. The great God Lydia looked like a disgruntled nun with her head swathed in bandages that way.

The doctor was leaving and taking Lydia with him. He wanted her to come to his office for an electroencephalogram test and X-rays. From what he could see she only had a minor skull fracture but it was best to make sure there was no concussion.

Lydia asked the doctor to wait in the hall for a minute while she spoke to Allison.

She closed the door carefully behind the doctor and came back into the bedroom.

"Listen to me and listen carefully," she warned Allison. "I'm letting you off easy. I talked to Paul and he advised me that if this story got out it could influence my trial. So I'm not going to press charges.

"I told the doctor that I got up in the middle of the night and slipped on the throw rug beside the bed. I said that I hit my head on the clock-radio as I fell. And that when you saw me lying on the floor with blood coming out of my head, you fainted.

"If anyone asks you any questions, just stick to that story. Do you understand?"

"I understand."

"All right, make sure you don't say anything else," Lydia went on. "Now, as far as you and I are concerned, I'm letting you get away with this to save my own skin, not yours. Believe me, nothing would give me greater pleasure than to see you behind bars on an assault and battery charge. But I can't afford the luxury of pressing charges against you while my own case is waiting to come up for trial.

"However, your little act last night finished things off between us for good. I've taken a lot from you, my love, but bashing my skull in was going a bit far. Don't you agree?" Lydia smiled. Rather, she twisted her lips into an expression that would have made a rattlesnake die of heart failure.

"This is it between us, cookie," Lydia continued. "I'll be gone for a couple of hours. I don't want to find you here when I get back.

"I'll be more definite about it." She glanced at her wristwatch. "It's eight o'clock now. I'll be back by eleven. When I get here, I want to find you gone. I don't want to know that you ever lived here. Take everything with you. If I find anything of yours still here, I'll burn it. Is that clear?"

"Quite clear."

"Allison," Lydia stopped and looked hard at the face of the girl who had shared her life for over a year. When she spoke again her voice had softened, a trace of tender regret softened her words. "I never loved you, Allison. I'm sure you knew that. I can't love anyone. But I cared for you in my own way. We had fun together. I'm sorry it had to end this way."

Allison burst into tears. "I'm sorry too," she sobbed.

Her tears did something to Lydia. The softness vanished and her voice became brittle and cruel again. "Cut the theatricals. I've got to leave now." She got up.

When she reached the French doors dividing the bedroom from the rest of the apartment, Lydia turned around. She dug in her pocket and pulled out a few bills. She placed one on top of the dresser. "Here's ten dollars. I believe that's what they give criminals when they let them go.

"Goodbye, Allison. And remember: I never want to see or hear from you again!"

Cal Staton was about to press the buzzer when he saw a man and woman coming down the steps. He waited until they opened the door then slipped his foot inside so the door would remain open behind them. As soon as they got out of his way, he dashed into the building and up the stairs.

The door to the apartment was open. Cal knocked once for politeness' sake then, receiving no answer, he rushed in.

He heard the sound of someone crying in the bedroom and followed the sound.

Allison was lying in the middle of the bed, sobs wracking through her. She was writhing on the bed in an agony of grief, plucking at the spread with shaking hands.

Cal sat down beside her and gathered her in his arms. Instinctively, he rocked her back and forth in the age old movement of comforting. Gradually, her sobs subsided.

"Baby, baby! Oh Allison, darling. Baby, what happened? Why are you crying?"

She looked at him blankly, as if she didn't recognize him. Then a hoarse cry came tearing out of the back of her throat. She wrapped her arms around Cal and pressed herself against him.

"I love you, Cal," Allison groaned as if it were delicious agony to say it. "I love you so very much."

Cal hugged her to him and kissed the tears off her face tenderly. "Allison ... oh, Allison, I love you."

When she had calmed down some more he asked her again what had happened.

She told him. Starting with Lydia's arrest and how she had felt responsible for it and that's why she had sent him away. And about learning that Lydia was having an affair with her cell-mate, Anne. She told him how this made her realize what a fool she had been and how she had gone to his apartment but he hadn't answered the door.

Cal interrupted her here. He explained what he had thought when Nancy gave him her message. He told her how he had gotten angry and thought she was playing games with him.

Then Allison told him the rest of what had happened. She told him about Sandy and about coming home and finding Lydia. And then she told him about last night. About Lydia's hitting her with the belt and how she had fractured Lydia's skull with the radio.

Allison started crying again.

"Don't cry, baby. Everything's going to be all right now. You're coming home with me."

"I can't," she wailed.

"What do you mean you can't?"

"I love you, Cal. I can't hurt you. You don't know me, Cal. I'm bad to the people I love. I hurt them."

"Of all the stupid things I've ever heard!" Cal checked himself. This was no time to get angry. "I need you with me, Allison."

"No, Cal. I'm no good. I'm sick. I'd be a burden to you. And besides, "Allison gulped as a fresh storm of tears came, "I've only got ten dollars."

He couldn't help laughing. "Honey," he managed to say at last, "I don't remember asking about your dowry."

She looked at him uncomprehendingly. "Dowry?" she squeaked.

"Oh, I forgot to tell you. You're marrying me."

"Marrying?"

"Yes, marrying. And if you've got any objections, tell me about them later. We'll have the rest of our lives to argue about it."

"I can think of far better things for us to do with our time than argue."

"Yeah, me too."

They smiled at each other in perfect understanding.

Cal stood up abruptly. "No time for that now. You stay in bed. Tell me where your suitcases and things are and I'll do the packing. We better hurry or Madam Lydia will be back before were finished."

Allison grabbed his hand. "We'll have time. There's something I want you to do for me before we start packing."

"Anything you want. You know I'll do anything for you."

She tried to stand up but the raw wounds on her back hurt too much. She fell back down on the bed. Cal was beside her instantly.

"Oh baby, I didn't know it hurt that badly. Did the doctor put anything on it?"

She shook her head no.

"Better put some Vaseline or something on it for now. We'll call a doctor as soon as we get to my place." He got up and went into the bathroom.

Presently, Cal returned with a jar of ointment. "Turn over," he instructed her.

Allison turned beet red. She remained on her back.

"This is no time for you to start getting modest! I've already seen your bottom, remember? I think you've got the prettiest behind in the world. I love your behind. In fact, I'm going to marry it. Now, will you please turn over."

Still blushing furiously, Allison turned over onto her stomach.

Cal sat down on the bed. He uncapped the jar of ointment and lifted Allison's nightgown. He groaned.

"I didn't know it was this bad. Oh baby, it must be horribly painful." His voice became charged with hate. "I'll kill her for doing this to you. So help me God, I'll kill her with my bare hands."

"Don't, Cal. Don't even think such things. Lydia is dead already. She's dead to both of us and that's all that matters."

He nodded in silent agreement and began spreading the ointment. Every time Allison winced, Cal felt the pain shooting through him. He would have given anything if he could have been the one who was hurt instead of Allison.

He finished, put the cap back on the jar of ointment and started to stand up.

"Hey, where are you going?"

"To pack your clothes."

"Uh uh," Allison remonstrated. "You promised to do something else first. You said you'd do anything I wanted."

"O. k."

Allison rolled over onto her back again. Her eyes were shining brightly. "Come here, darling," she whispered softly.

Desire flamed through him. He fought to keep himself under control. "Your back ... the pain ..."

"I won't mind the pain. It won't really hurt. Cal, please ... oh, please."

He tore his clothes off and left them lying on the floor. He knelt on the bed and gathered her gently in his arms. The touch of her lips on his drove him into a frenzy. The tip of her tongue darted against his.

A wild passion surged through Allison. She tore her mouth from his and tossed her head back. She laughed throatily, a laugh of triumph and desire.

UNNATURAL

Cal's lips trailed over her throat and down to the swelling mounds bursting above her nightgown. She grabbed the gown on either side of his face and pulled. The flimsy material tore apart easily.

He felt the heavy sag of her breasts in his hands and buried his face between them. Murmuring her name, he reveled in the silky feel of them.

Allison responded with a wild, ardent hunger. She offered herself to him completely. It was as if she had become a virgin again and was experiencing passion for the first, crazy, sweet, wonderful, overwhelming time.

She was suspended somewhere in a world of impossible beauty and it couldn't last because it was too good, too good. But it got better and better...and so wonderful she couldn't stand it...and she was too happy...and it was slipping, slipping...falling away...gently...gently...oh so gently...falling...and he was marvelous...and she belonged to him...and then they were both melting together...and flowing out...out...down...into delight.

Later, when the delicious langour was fading away, Cal got up and packed Allison's clothes for her.

Allison lay on the bed alone. This was the time when her thoughts always became agonizingly clear. The time after the blinding heat of passion when she faced the horrible mess that was her life.

She heard Cal swear to himself as he dropped a loaded suitcase on his foot.

She smiled. So good to hear his voice, to know he was in the next room.

Cal would always be near her. From now on. For always. Allison sipped the wild sweet wine of happiness.

www.ingramcontent.com/pod-product-compliance
Lightning Source LLC
Chambersburg PA
CBHW030345180626
46812CB00007B/2762